Drina
Dances
Alone

Jean Estoril

Illustrated by Jenny Sanders

AN
APPLE
PAPERBACK

SCHOLASTIC INC.
New York Toronto London Auckland Sydney

The illustrator would like to acknowledge the
help of Cathy Marston, the young dancer,
and her teacher Maureen Mitchell,
of the Eden Dance Centre in Cambridge.

ISBN 0-590-43081-5

12 11 10 9 8 7 6 5 4 3 2 1   9/8 0 1 2 3 4/9

Printed in the U.S.A.   11

First Scholastic printing, June 1989

A Note to Readers

Drina Dances Alone is set in England. A few of the British places and terms you may not be familiar with are listed below.

Cockney — a person from one area of London; also a type of speech.
Covent Garden — London's opera house, and the home of the Royal Ballet.
flat — an apartment.
the lift — an elevator.
Stalls Circle — the first balcony in a theater; usually the best seats in the house.
the Tube — the London subway.

Here are some ballet terms you may not know:

arabesque — a ballet pose in which the dancer stands on one leg and stretches the other leg high in back.

barre — a bar attached to the wall which dancers use to maintain their balance.

battement — a kick.

corps de ballet — literally means "the body of the ballet"; chorus or the ensemble dancers.

divertissements — solo pieces within a ballet, which usually have nothing to do with the story of the ballet.

pas de deux — literally means "a step for two."

pirouette — movement in place in which the dancer turns while keeping his or her weight on one foot.

plié — to bend at the knees.

port de bras — the movement of a dancer's arm from one position to another.

CONTENTS

BOOK ONE
Ballet in Buckinghamshire

1

The Sleeping Beauty

"Covent Garden!" Drina cried, leaping to her feet as the train slid to a standstill and the doors opened.

Rose Conway, her great friend from the Dominick Ballet School, followed her in a rather more leisurely way.

"It's quite early, Drina. There's no need to rush. The curtain won't go up for more than twenty minutes."

"Oh, I know. But I do love to be in my seat as early as possible. It's such fun to watch other people arriving and to have time to – to savour it all," Drina said, as they squeezed their way into the lift.

"It is, of course," Rose agreed, her usually pale face flushed after the heat of the train. "And, anyway, we've got to get up to the amphitheatre."

"And we've never seen *The Sleeping Beauty*. Oh, Rose, isn't it lovely to live in London and to be able to go to the Royal Opera House on Saturday afternoons?"

Rose nodded. She had lived in London all her life and could not really imagine living anywhere else, but Drina had spent a number of years in Willerbury, a Warwickshire town, and had come to live in Westminster with her grandparents eighteen months before, when she was almost twelve.

Both girls wore the attractive grey and scarlet uniform of the Dominick School, and the vivid red suited Drina in particular, for she was very dark, taking after her Italian father.

The lift gates opened and they stepped eagerly out into the cold January afternoon, crossed the road and hurried down Floral Street.

To Drina it was all familiar enough now, but she never failed to get a thrill from the grey streets round the Royal Opera House. But now her whole mind was on the ballet they were going to see. She knew a great deal of the music and the thought that, so soon, the curtain would go up on the Princess Aurora's christening made her scalp prickle with excitement. The theatre was in her blood, for her mother had been a very great dancer, Elizabeth Ivory. It was only a year since Drina had learned the astonishing fact, for her grandparents,who had not wished her to follow in her mother's footsteps, had kept it from her as long as possible. Not even Rose knew the truth, for Drina had vowed that she would succeed on her own, without the help of being known as Ivory's daughter. Mrs Pilgrim and Jenny, her friends in Willerbury, knew the truth, and so did Mr Colin Amberdown, a ballet critic, and Adele Whiteway, a grown-up friend of Drina's, but to everyone at the Dominick School she was just Drina Adams, a hard-working thirteen-year-old who showed, perhaps, no more talent than anyone else. Even the recent chance that she had had to dance in a West End play had not spoilt Drina, for she was very humble and she knew that only years of hard work could make her into a good dancer.

Rose gave a cry of protest as Drina hurried on, round

the corner to the front of the Opera House.

"Oh, Drina! Where are you *going*? We don't go in at the front!"

Drina groped in her shoulder-bag and waved two tickets triumphantly.

"We do, then. I wanted to give you a surprise. We're not in the amphitheatre this time, seeing the stage all funny from near the roof. We're at the front of the Stalls Circle."

Still a trifle bewildered, Rose pushed her way through the crowd in the entrance hall.

"I know you sit in good seats when you go with your grandmother. But I can't afford the Stalls Circle, Drina. Honestly, you know I can't. You *said* you'd get amphitheatre——"

"I meant to, but Granny said she was sorry not to be able to take me and the seats are a treat for both of us. And I'm so glad, because I don't want to miss a single thing."

"It's really nice of your granny," said Rose. Unlike Drina, she was not well off, and though her father and mother were very proud of her and were quite convinced that she would be a famous dancer one day, they could not afford expensive theatre seats. "Oh, isn't it thrilling? The Opera House looks quite different from here." And they stood for a moment absorbing the atmosphere of the vast place, until the people behind them urged them on good-humouredly and a programme seller came to show them to their seats.

They opened their programmes at once, intent on discovering who was to dance each part, and for five minutes neither spoke. Then Rose said:

"Your granny's a dear, isn't she? At first I was rather scared of her, but she's really so very kind."

Drina nodded, tossing back her smooth, black hair.

"Do you know, I was a bit scared of her once, even though she's brought me up since I was a baby and is almost like my mother. But since she's let me dance she's been quite different. She's worried just now, though, and I said we'd get our own tea when we go back, if she's busy."

"Is your grandfather still ill?" Rose asked sympathetically.

"Yes. He's had bronchitis very badly and Granny told me last night that the doctor isn't satisfied. Grandfather's had a lot of colds and coughs this winter, and then, this last week, he's been really bad. Granny said he ought to get out of England to a warmer place for a time, but she didn't seem to think it would be possible. I didn't even realise," added Drina guiltily, "that his coughs were serious. There's been such a lot to think about this winter——"

"I know," Rose agreed. "Working so hard at the Dominick and then your being in *Argument in Paris*. After all, it's only a fortnight since it finished. I thought you'd be awfully miserable because the play didn't run, but you don't seem to be."

Drina stared very hard at the heavy red curtains.

"I did mind. I had a struggle with myself at first. But all that really matters is working at the Dominick. Only I feel mean because I didn't even know until last night that Granny was really upset and worried."

Then she studied her programme again until the lights went down and the overture began, and then she had thoughts only for the satisfying moment. How thrilling it always was before the curtain rose! How wonderful to be in the Royal Opera House, waiting for *The Sleeping Beauty* to begin!

As the curtains parted she sat slightly forward in her seat, her hands tightly clasped and her mouth dry with excitement. And from then on, with her eyes never moving from the great stage, she was under almost as great a spell as the Wicked Fairy was to put on the Princess Aurora. She was quite lost in the world of ballet, where Cattalabutte, Master of the Ceremonies, looked so splendid and the fairies danced. The Fairy of the Crystal Fountain, the Fairy of the Enchanted Garden, the Fairy of the Woodland Glade . . . and, of course, the Fairy of the Lilac, with her own beautiful tune, who was to save the Princess from death and cause her, as well as the whole Court, to sleep for a hundred years.

"One day," thought Drina fleetingly, as the music filled the great theatre, "one day it might be me." But she knew that when the time came for her to go on some stage in *The Sleeping Beauty* it was far more likely to be as some humble page or attendant than as the Lilac Fairy.

At the end of the Prologue there was an interval, but they were both too much held in the atmosphere of the ballet to talk, and soon the curtain rose again on the Princess Aurora's sixteenth birthday festivities. Watching the famous ballerina dancing the Rose Adagio, Drina was so filled with delight that sharp tears pricked her eyes. Such perfect movements . . . such a perfect body and complete control . . . That was what they were all striving for every day at the *barre* at the Dominick School. And then, once again, she forgot everything but the complete ballet before her – the colour and music and movement and the fairy story that was so familiar.

The long act went on. The Lilac Fairy cast her spell

and gradually sleep came to everyone, the forest grew up about the Palace and the curtain came softly down.

"Oh, Drina!" cried Rose, clasping her friend's hand.

Drina came back to earth with difficulty, blinking the shameful tears from her lashes.

"It's a good thing it's *you*," she said, knowing that Rose had noticed but was not, in any case, quite dry-eyed herself. "Granny would be disgusted with me. She says I get too carried away. She doesn't approve a bit, and Jenny says it's an unreal, half-lit world. But I can't help it. I *do* try to criticise and note things all the time, but I keep on getting lost."

"So do I," Rose agreed. "But I try to watch properly, too, not just carried away in a dream. Oh, Drina, the Rose Adagio! We could never dance it like that in a hundred years."

"I know," Drina said soberly. "It makes me feel so humble I wonder we even try."

When the ballet was over they emerged, rather dazed, into the streets.

"Let's go home by bus," Drina suggested and they turned down Wellington Street towards the Strand, the January air gradually bringing them back to the real world.

"Let's walk," Rose said presently. "It isn't far and it's not very late. I couldn't eat any tea yet."

"I could," Drina admitted. "I've suddenly realised that I'm ravenous, and I told you we'd got to get it ready ourselves. Still, it won't take long. We'll go along the Embankment. I love it when all the lights are on."

Halfway between Waterloo and Westminster Bridges they stopped and leaned over the wall to look down at the dark river and at the lights on the other side.

"Oh, I do love London!" Drina exclaimed. "When we

first came I was miserable and I didn't really like it at all. But now I couldn't live anywhere else. There's always so much to see; so much going on."

"So many theatres," added Rose, looking back at the Igor Dominick Theatre on the other side of the road. "The Opera House is wonderful, but the Dominick is especially ours. I wonder if we'll ever get into the Company?"

"I suppose it's no use wondering," Drina remarked. "I can't imagine the future if we don't – one day. And I can't imagine it if we *do*. Just think of being a member of the Igor Dominick Company! Anyway, I think just now I'm content to be in London, and at the Dominick School."

"But you liked living in Warwickshire," said Rose as, shivering in the wind, they turned and hurried on towards Westminster. "And you like that farm you go to stay at with Jenny Pilgrim."

"Willerbury was all right," said Drina, looking back at that time as though it had been in another life. "And I started dancing at the Selswick Ballet School there. And the farm's all right, too, for a little while, though I'm not like Jenny. I really rather hate mud and animal smells, but Jenny says she's going to be a farmer. I'm not a country person. I'm a town mouse."

"We're both town mouses – I mean mice!" cried Rose and, giggling, they took to their heels and ran, until the traffic on the bridge made them pause.

Five minutes later they approached the large block of modern flats where Drina lived and went up in the lift. The air seemed very warm after the icy wind and their cheeks were glowing as Drina put her key into the front door of the flat.

Mrs Chester, Drina's grandmother, met them in the

hall. As usual her manner was extremely controlled and her grey hair was smartly dressed, but Drina noticed, with a sudden feeling of dismay, that her brow was unusually creased and there were dark shadows under her eyes.

"So you're back! I was beginning to worry. I suppose you walked, and you know I don't like you wandering about London after dark, Drina. How are you, Rose, dear?"

"Very well, thank you," said Rose. "And thank you very, very much for the lovely seats. You've no idea what a difference it makes to see the *whole* stage. The only time I ever go in good seats is when we're all taken to the Dominick, and then we get them cheap."

Mrs Chester smiled a trifle grimly.

"I have quite a good idea. In my own young days I often went in the gallery. You will both try to be quiet, won't you? Your grandfather is asleep, Drina. I've got your tea ready, since I had a little time. There isn't much to do, so I'll have a cup with you, though I had my tea some time ago."

"Oh, thank you, Granny," said Drina, and they went into Drina's bedroom to take off their outdoor clothes.

Drina stood by the bed for a moment, her face grave.

"Granny looks older than I thought she was, somehow. I feel rather a beast. Fancy going out and enjoying myself!"

"But she *wanted* you to," said Rose and, quietly, they went to the bathroom to wash their hands.

2

Bad News

To Drina's relief her grandfather was better sooner than the doctor and her grandmother seemed to have expected, and by the middle of February he was back at his office, though looking rather more frail than usual.

"If only the weather wasn't so abominable!" cried Mrs Chester one day, glancing out into the sleety rain. "Thank goodness, at least, that *you* seem strong enough now, Drina."

Drina leaned forward to "touch wood", though she was well aware that such a superstitious gesture would irritate her grandmother.

"I'm almost the only one in my class who hasn't been away this term. Rose missed a whole week with her cold and heaps of them have had flu."

"I certainly don't think Rose is very strong," said Mrs Chester. "She looks anæmic to me."

"Yes, they told her so when we had the medical examinations at the end of last term," Drina said worriedly. "I don't really know what it means. She's no paler than I am, but she does get tired, though she won't ever confess it."

"*Yours* is a healthy pallor. She's thoroughly peaky,"

said her grandmother.

Drina certainly felt full of energy, in spite of the cold, wet weather, and she flung herself into each day at the Dominick School with great zest. The school day always started with a ballet class and she really felt that she was making good progress. This was comforting knowledge, for her first two terms at the ballet school had been rather difficult. Many of her contemporaries had shown far greater promise and Drina had found life a struggle. Then, the previous term, she had seemed to catch up, in spite of the hard work she had to put into her part in the play, *Argument in Paris*.

She now felt able to hold her own with her old rival from Willerbury, Daphne Daniety, but Queenie Rothington was still the most showy member of their class. Drina sometimes sighed when she thought of Queenie. She was not jealous and she would have been ready enough to be friends with Queenie, but they had been enemies – on Queenie's side, at least – since their arrival at the Dominick more than a year before and things were little better now.

Still, Queenie's overbearing ways were a small trouble really, and Drina was happy and busy. The days passed all too quickly and she enjoyed most things. Very often the Juniors were taken to Art Galleries and concerts and sometimes there were mass visits to matinées at the Dominick Theatre, where the Company was well launched on the ballet season.

With Rose, a boy called Jan Williams, and several other friends, Drina was well content, but she never forgot to write to Jenny in Warwickshire. Jenny was someone very special, her oldest and dearest friend, even though she had long since given up her ballet lessons and was uncompromisingly critical of the ballet world.

"Come to us at Easter," Jenny wrote early in February. "You can count on me to provide the light relief. I'm sure you need a change from all those hopeful future ballerinas doing dreary exercises at the *barre* every day. I know you adore every single minute of it, but it's my mission in life to keep you anchored to something more down to earth. I went to the farm last weekend and there were quite a lot of lambs. Poor little things! It seems such a shame, when it's so cold and there was about a foot of snow in places.

"But, going back to ballet, I heard a bit of gossip through Joy Kelly the other day. She's in an awful state about it, actually, though there's another dancing school in the town and I suppose most of them will have to go there. The Selswick School is closing down at Easter. Madame has been ill and she's decided that the school is too much of a strain now that she's getting older. She's going to live in London and do part-time teaching at the Dominick, as well as being there in an advisory capacity, whatever that means. So you'll see her sometimes and may even be taught by her, and I suppose you'll like that. She wasn't a bad old stick, but I can only remember the Selswick with a shudder because of all those horrible *pliés* and *demi-pliés* and *battements* and *pirouettes* I did, just to please Mother."

Drina thought it rather irreverent of Jenny to call Miss Janetta Selswick an "old stick" when she had been so good-looking and graceful, but that was like Jenny. And it was true that her lessons at the Selswick School had been endured entirely to please her mother, who had once cherished dreams of possessing a daughter who was a famous ballerina.

The news that Madame was to join the Dominick

School was very welcome and was soon confirmed by Adele Whiteway.

"Janetta Selswick? Oh, yes, it's quite true. She'll be attached to the Dominick next term. That ballet school of hers has had a wonderful reputation, but I know she isn't all that strong and probably she's eager to get back to London. She *is* a Londoner, of course."

"It will be strange but nice to see her there next term," said Drina.

So the term went on and it was almost March. Drina was so well occupied and her head was so filled with affairs at the Dominick and in the ballet world generally, that she scarcely noticed the slight disturbance in her own home. Her grandmother seemed busier than usual and her brow was nearly always puckered. She wrote a great many letters and was frequently out on mysterious errands.

Drina simply had a vague, uneasy feeling that things were not quite the same as usual, but when she did, in the end, ask her grandmother, "Is something the matter? Are you worrying about anything?" Mrs Chester said rather shortly:

"Not really worried, no. But I'm very busy." And, since it was not her way to confide much in her granddaughter, Drina supposed that she would hear in good time and at least her grandfather seemed much better, though he had rather a preoccupied air.

Then, one evening at the beginning of March, Mrs Chester said:

"Drina, put away your books and come and sit over here. We've got something to tell you." Her voice was much as usual, but her face was grave, and Drina saw with a suddenly leaping heart that her grandfather, too, looked as though something important and possibly not very pleasant was pending. She pushed her books together, dropped her history book, and tossed back her swinging hair. Fear, sharp and unexpected, shot through her and suddenly she knew that she ought to have realised that something was afoot. In fact, she *had* known, at the very back of her mind, and had not been able to face the knowledge.

"Sit down on your stool," said Mrs Chester, pushing it over to her, but Drina generally preferred to sit on the floor near one of the radiators on cold nights, and the night was very cold indeed, with wild storm clouds and flurries of sleet against the windows.

She sat down with a grace that was absolutely natural to her and clasped her hands round her knees. As she looked from one face to the other the frightened feeling grew.

"What is it? Is it something terrible?"

"You always exaggerate so," said her grandmother, in her cool, controlled voice. "No, it isn't *terrible*, though you will probably feel a little sad and upset. But we're counting on you to help us by being as sensible as you can. You know I told you that your grandfather ought to get out of England?"

"Yes." Drina's fingers tightened round her knees until her bones were white against the thin flesh.

Mrs Chester looked across at her husband.

"You'd better tell her."

"The firm has asked me to go to Australia for several months," Mr Chester said quietly. "I shall be dealing with important business matters, but it will be a holiday as well, so we are going by sea, and the doctor strongly advises me to go. So you see——"

Drina felt that there was a hard lump in her throat

and her back was so tense that it ached. She couldn't speak and was glad when her grandmother took up the tale again.

"I don't want him to go alone, Drina. If you had been younger, of course there would have been no question of my going, unless we'd taken you with us, but now you're thirteen and a half, and old enough to understand and bear a change." She glanced at Drina's blank, stricken face and went on hurriedly, "My dear, the decision has cost me a lot of thought. You've never been separated from us before, except for very short periods, but we did always plan to send you to boarding-school for a time——"

There was a singing in Drina's ears and she wondered if she were going to faint. They were going far across the world without her – that was bad enough – but what, oh, what, was going to happen to *her*? What about the Dominick and her dancing? It was worse, ten thousand times worse, than that evening when she had learned that they were leaving Willerbury and that she might not dance again.

Her voice seemed to come from very far away:

"I don't understand, Granny! Where shall I go? What shall I do?"

"At first we did think of taking you with us, but it would mean interrupting your education as well as your dancing. The dancing I'm not keen about even now, as you know, but it would break your heart to stop your lessons for so long——"

A solution came to Drina in a flash.

"Couldn't I – couldn't I go to Miss Whiteway? She'd have me, I know, even though her niece lives with her in term-time. There's a little spare room——"

"She would have had you," her grandmother said

quickly. "But you forget that she's going to Paris with the Dominick Company, and then on to Spain and several other countries."

"She's designed the sets for two of the new ballets," Drina said faintly. "I'd forgotten. But she won't be away so very long. When – when are you going to Australia?"

This was the moment that Mrs Chester had dreaded, though she believed that children should be kept in ignorance of adult plans until they were on the point of being carried out.

"Rather soon, I'm afraid. In less than a fortnight. We've got a passage and there seems no point in delaying. The flat will be sublet for six months, and then perhaps for another three or six months, depending on how things work out, and——"

"But the Dominick?" It was an agonised cry, though Drina was fighting hard for composure. She recognised well enough, even in the midst of her bewilderment and fright, that her grandmother was suffering, too.

"You needn't worry about your dancing. That is all taken care of. I went out to Buckinghamshire last week and it's all arranged. You're to be a boarder at the Dominick Residential School – Chalk Green Manor. Don't you remember you once saw it from the outside, you and Rose?"

"We just went to the gates," Drina gasped. "It was right in the heart of the country. Miles and miles from London."

"Actually it's not forty miles from London and it's in a wonderfully healthy place. I was most favourably impressed with it, and all the students looked very healthy and happy. You'll be well cared for there and a summer in the country will do you a world of good."

Drina was utterly silent. The residential school! The students who sometimes came in private buses to matinées in London, wearing emerald green and grey uniforms instead of scarlet and grey ones! She had always pitied them as beings from another world, cut off from the real world of London and the ballet school in Red Lion Square.

"But——"

"It really is a lovely place, Drina," said Mr Chester. "We hate to leave you, but you'll be brave and soon you'll find yourself happy in the country."

"I hate the country!" cried Drina and then, when she saw their faces, she could have bitten out her tongue.

"Mrs Pilgrim will be your guardian while we're away," Mrs Chester went on quietly. "It's unfortunate that you have no aunts or cousins in this country, but Mrs Pilgrim is a balanced, sensible woman on the whole, and Jenny will be delighted to have you in the holidays. If you're ill or in any difficulty Mrs Pilgrim will deal with it, and she'll buy your clothes and give you your pocket-money. And, of course, in any dire emergency one or both of us could fly back to you in a very short time. Now go and get your milk. It's past your bedtime."

Drina, used to the habit of obedience, rose at once, but she felt that milk would choke her. She had even totally forgotten that she had been going to ask to see a ballet programme on the television. It was *Petrouchka*,* a ballet she had never seen.

"The time will go very quickly," her grandfather almost pleaded as he took up *The Times* again and Drina got herself out of the room somehow. She did not go to the kitchen, but up to her own room, where she locked the door and flung herself on her bed. For

---

several moments misery and fierce, selfish rebellion possessed her, so that she did not notice the wind howling outside.

"Oh, I shall die! I really shall! The Dominick . . . and London . . . and Rose. And Miss Selswick coming next term. I can't be an exile. I'd much sooner be dead. And Granny and Grandfather so far away!"

But she had developed a great deal mentally lately, even though her body was still so small and slight, and she had unconsciously learned control from her grandmother's example. Besides, she really did love them both very much and it was no good distressing them further. So after ten minutes or so, during which no one came to disturb her, she got up, washed her face and went quietly down to fetch her milk and biscuits. Back in the sitting-room she asked in a slightly breathless voice, "When shall I have to – go?"

"A week today," her grandmother told her. "Next Tuesday. I'll take you, of course. And your green scarf and blouses are on order. Oh, and your new cloak. They have them lined with emerald green, of course, at Chalk Green. You'll have to help to sew nametapes on all your new things, won't you?"

"Y-yes."

"And I'll pack a large suitcase with all your summer clothes and send it off to Willerbury. You won't need them during the rest of this term, that's certain. There'll be less than a month of it, though Easter is late. It's going to be a busy time, Drina, and I'm sure that your teachers will excuse you from homework for the rest of this week. I'll write a note for you to take tomorrow."

It was a relief to go back to her room, but after a few minutes there was a knock at the door and her grandfather came in.

"Drina, my dear, it's been a great blow, I know. I wanted to tell you sooner, but you know your grandmother well enough by now."

"I – I'll get used to the idea," Drina said with difficulty and suddenly flung her arms round his neck. "I do want you to get really well again and it'll be so lovely and warm and sunny, won't it?"

"That's the idea," he said, more cheerfully. Then he handed her several folded five-pound notes. "Buy yourself some new ballet books to take with you, or a new make-up box, or whatever you like. You're a brave girl."

But Drina cried herself to sleep and dreamed wildly for what seemed the whole night. She was standing outside the Dominick School in Red Lion Square and the door was closed against her. She knocked and rang until she was exhausted, but no one came, and the board with the gold lettering had gone. Then she was down by the river and there was no Dominick Theatre, and when she asked someone about it the woman looked blank and assured her that there had never been such a theatre.

She awoke at seven o'clock to the knowledge that there had been some truth in the dreams. She was to be cut off from the Dominick, far away in the remote beechwoods of Buckinghamshire. There would still be dancing lessons, it was true, but with a new teacher, amongst strange students. There would be none of the stimulus of being in such close contact with the Company. No chance to watch them leaving the rehearsal room next door to the Dominick School; no hope of seeing Marianne Volonaise or Igor Dominick about the building.

"But they *visit* Chalk Green," she told herself as she dressed. "I know they do." And she put on a brave face during breakfast, though it cost her an enormous effort.

It was a relief to run off to catch her bus.

The news of Drina's imminent departure was received by Rose and her other friends with deepest dismay and sympathy, but Daphne Daniety actually laughed and Queenie Rothington said loudly:

"Our little Drina going into exile! Fancy! I'd hate to go to Chalk Green myself. Horrible little goody-goodies they always look, being shepherded to London about once a month. *I'm* never happy unless I'm in the thick of things."

"Oh, do shut up!" cried Rose. "You always were a beast, Queenie! Drina hates the very idea."

"She looks like a dying duck," said Queenie nastily. "*Not* the Dying Swan. Pavlova will never be *her* middle name!" And she went off with Jill and Betty, who admired her but often wished she would not say such very unpleasant things.

After the ballet class Miss Lane, the headmistress, sent for Drina, and she looked with some pity at the set, pale face of her pupil.

"I'm very sorry to hear that we're to lose you, Drina," she said kindly. "But it will only be for two or three terms and then you'll be back with us. Chalk Green Manor is a fine place – absolutely up-to-date, and with splendid teachers. And you'll love the Chiltern country. I come from near High Wycombe myself and when I was your age I delighted in the woods and hills and the lonely 'bottoms' and hamlets. Even the names are a delight – Summer Heath and

Christmas Common, Lacey Green, Hampdenleaf Wood, Bix Bottom, Lily Bottom. You'll love them all, especially in summer. And in autumn, too. Autumn in the Chilterns is always wonderful, and the Chalk Green students are really very free. After the first few days you'll be very happy."

"Yes, Miss Lane. Thank you," Drina said dutifully, but the hard lump was still in her throat and misery seemed to have her in an iron grip.

She did not go to her classroom immediately, but stood at an upstairs window, staring out into Red Lion Square. And suddenly she remembered another high window, a window at the Selswick School where she had stood and faced the knowledge that she might never dance again.

That had been a bad time, but in the end things had turned out well. She had come to the Dominick and learned to love London. She had made new friends and been happy.

But optimism seemed to have deserted her and she could only think of the hills of Buckinghamshire with bleak despair. Who wanted Hampdenleaf Wood and places called Bix Bottom and Christmas Common when they could have Piccadilly Circus, and Shaftesbury Avenue with its theatres; all the splendid, exciting pageant of London?

3

Ballet Boarding School

It was a nightmare week, all the more so because Drina tried so hard to hide her deep unhappiness from her grandparents. The thing was arranged and nothing could alter it. So, with every bit of character she possessed, she tried to show a brave and even a cheerful face. It was the hardest thing she had ever done, but to a large extent she succeeded. Her grandmother seemed to be deceived, though her grandfather was not. But he really believed that she would be happy at Chalk Green as soon as the first strangeness had passed. Drina was convinced that she would never be happy again, but that was her problem, to be faced in secret in the dark, night after night.

She was very proud and pride, in the end, was a help. After the first shock she could not bear to show her sorrow and fear at the Dominick School. Queenie and Daphne were glad that she was going; others lamented her fate. To both Drina learned to present a calm, pale face, and only the faithful Rose knew the depths of her emotion.

"Nothing will be the same without you," she said when they were alone, wandering home from school.

Generally they walked as far as Piccadilly Circus together, when Rose took the Tube to Earls Court and Drina plunged down Lower Regent Street and through St James's Park to Westminster. "Oh, Drina, I wish you weren't going!"

"I'd give everything on earth not to be going," said Drina. But it wasn't true. Her grandparents' happiness came first and the moment she reached the flat she fought hard to be cheerful and ordinary, helping with the many tasks that piled on her grandmother during the last days.

Jan Williams, the boy who had been friendly with Drina for a year, was sympathetic but reassuring.

"Honestly, Drina, you'll like it. Of course it *is* cut off, in a way, but my little cousin loves it. I told you we sometimes visit her there, and she spends her holidays with us, because her parents are abroad. Her name's Bronwen Jones. She's only eleven, but a very sensible kid and quite a good dancer. I'll write and tell her you're going. She can show you round and tell you everything."

Drina thanked him warmly, but felt that eleven-year-old Bronwen Jones was unlikely to be much comfort in an alien world. She tried to tell herself that it would not be as strange as all that, that the dancing classes would be the same and that everyone would have the same aims, but it did not help much. The thought of the empty countryside all about Chalk Green Manor oppressed her. Though the farm in Warwickshire was much farther from London, her brief glimpse of Chalk Green had left her with an impression of utter remoteness. Hills and deep woods and tiny villages. Chalk Green itself was just a cluster of brick and flint cottages round a small triangle of grass; not even a church or a village school, or, at any rate, she had not noticed them.

As the days passed Drina found herself seeing London anew; everything seemed important, sharply outlined. Everything gave her delight, a delight so painful that it was almost unbearable. The sound of Big Ben, the towers of Westminster against the wild sunsets, the traffic swirling round Piccadilly Circus, the faint green buds on the trees in the parks. The sound of Cockney voices . . . the smell of the river on a wet evening . . . the endless posters that advertised coming events, plays, ballets and concerts.

In London life never stopped – there was always something. And she was going away. It didn't matter that the journey was less than forty miles. It might just as well have been five hundred.

"To think I was ever miserable here!" Drina thought as she returned home from school on Friday afternoon. The parting with the Dominick was over. She had dressed for the last time in the familiar cloakrooms and walked through the hall, past her mother's portrait and her ballet shoes in the glass case. By the time she saw them again she would be fourteen. But she could not imagine the future; it seemed dark and bleak.

At the weekend the weather turned suddenly springlike. The sun shone almost with warmth and the street traders' barrows were one solid mass of gold – gold of daffodils and jonquils heaped together. On Sunday afternoon Drina and Rose walked on Hampstead Heath and even sunned themselves for a time in a warm hollow. Then they tramped on towards Kenwood House and Drina paid a farewell visit to some of her favourite pictures, including "Little Miss

Murray".

"You must come and stay with us for a weekend soon," said Rose as they parted. She was not going back to the flat for tea as Mrs Chester was still so busy. "If you wouldn't mind sleeping in my room, that is."

"I wouldn't mind a bit," Drina assured her fervently and they took their leave hurriedly, both suddenly a trifle shy. They had not realised how fond they were of each other until the knowledge of parting.

On Monday Drina's packing was finished and all the last minute things attended to. Her school trunk had already been sent off and her suitcase stood in the hall, a constant reminder, if one were needed, of imminent departure.

Drina felt unlike herself, somehow detached and cold. Even her hands were icy cold, though the day was surprisingly warm.

There had been a letter from Jenny that morning.

"I know you'll feel like dying, but I'm looking forward to the Easter holidays no end. And it will be great to have you for nearly two months in the summer. Mother's planning to rent a cottage in the Welsh mountains. That might be rather fun, don't you think? We can study farming in Wales a bit, perhaps. Mostly sheep, I suppose." How like Jenny that was! "You probably *will* like Chalk Green when you get used to it, and aren't there lots of foreigners there? That ought to be awfully interesting. I shall be thinking about you a lot."

And she would, too. Jenny was warm-hearted and very understanding, and to her Drina had always been able to pour out her heart.

In the early afternoon the telephone bell rang and Drina gathered at once that it was her grandfather speaking. Her grandmother was saying:

"Oh, well, I suppose so, though I'm up to my eyes in our own packing and planning how to leave the flat. Yes, I've no doubt she will enjoy it, though an early night would be better for her. There are shadows under her eyes."

However, the matter was evidently arranged and Drina felt a sudden glow of excitement when Mrs Chester said, as she left the telephone:

"We're going to that Spanish Ballet Company at the Queen Elizabeth Theatre. Your grandfather thought you'd like it. You haven't seen any Spanish dancing, have you?"

"No. I'd just love to go, Granny!" Drina cried and for a time, at least, her misery abated somewhat.

She had not been inside the Queen Elizabeth Theatre since January 11th, when *Argument in Paris* was acted for the last time, and it felt strange to be in the Circle, looking at the heavy blue curtains. How well she knew what it was like backstage, though it seemed a long time since she had been there. So much had happened in the weeks between.

Soon the old spell was on her and she sat with clasped hands waiting for the curtain to rise. And, though it was so very different from classical ballet, the Spanish dancing filled her with warmth and pleasure; excitement, too, so that her cheeks burned and her heart raced. The colour of the women's costumes was so superb and their dark grace held her spellbound. The rhythmic clicking of the castanets, the strange, wild flamenco singing, the stamping of the men's heels on the stage. . . . In some ways it was the most exciting thing she had ever seen.

The fact that by the next night she would be at Chalk

Green Manor was momentarily forgotten and her grandfather glanced at her rapt face with satisfaction. It had distressed him deeply to see her brave, forced cheerfulness.

As they drove home to Westminster the streets were shining with rain and the wind was so cold that the spring weather seemed a dream.

"But there'll soon be primroses and violets in the Chiltern woods," said Mrs Chester.

The next morning came the terrible parting from her grandfather and the flat, and Drina felt hardly real at all as the taxi sped through the wet streets to Marylebone Station. She wore her new emerald green scarf and an emerald blouse, with her grey school suit and big coat, and her luggage bore bright green labels: "Miss Drina Adams, Chalk Green Manor, near High Wycombe, Bucks". In her coat pocket was her dearest possession, a small black cat called Hansl, her mother's own mascot in the days when she had been a great ballerina.

Mrs Chester was very silent, the station was cold and dreary, and the train had no corridor into which Drina could escape. So she sat with clasped hands, her dark hair swinging slightly forward to hide her face, ignoring the magazines that had been bought at the bookstall. In less than an hour the train would reach High Wycombe. In two hours her grandmother would probably have started on her return journey to London and the long exile would have started.

The rain stopped just as the fields began, but the sky was grey and there was nothing about the scene to make Drina feel any more cheerful, though she was still doing her best to look calm and at ease. For a time there were woods and fields and cows standing rather

sadly in the mud by five-barred gates, then there were buildings again and a wide main road, and houses climbing up the hills on either side.

"Be sure we don't leave anything!" Mrs Chester said anxiously. "At least we haven't got to worry about your trunk, but there's the suitcase, the holdall, your raincoat and your new radio."

Drina seized the raincoat and the radio, a present from her grandmother, and hitched her shoulder-bag into place. Her hands were icy cold in spite of her fur-lined gloves.

Mrs Chester looked for a taxi to take them to Chalk Green Manor on the slopes of Bledlow Ridge. They soon found one and sped off through the town and along the main road towards West Wycombe. Then along a valley beside the railway, where the hills on either hand were covered with beechwoods. The woods, Drina noticed, were, even in the grey light, not black, but sometimes almost purple-blue and sometimes a faint red-gold. But the fact gave her no pleasure.

"Beech is so late coming out," said Mrs Chester, almost absently. "You won't see them at their best until May. That larchwood is a most beautiful colour."

So it was the larches that were darkish red. Drina stored away the scrap of knowledge, for she was conscious that she knew very little about country things, in spite of Jenny. Probably the students at the Manor knew a great deal.

They passed the charming village of Bradenham, with its brick-and-flint cottages with their russet roofs, its church and manor-house dreaming round the big green, and soon turned up a lane on the left that Drina half-remembered. How happy and carefree she had been on that day last summer when they had driven out into the Chiltern country!

"We've said most things," said Mrs Chester suddenly. "Be a good, sensible girl, Drina, and write at least once a week. You've got the supply of air-letters? And remember that Australia isn't far away nowadays. In real trouble we could be back very quickly: that should comfort you. Though there probably won't *be* any real trouble. I devoutly hope not."

"No. I mean yes, Granny," Drina said with difficulty.

There were scarcely any houses now and the ridge and the thick woods loomed darkly. Chalk Green was hidden almost until they were upon the first cottages and then it was gone in a flash. The car was turning in at big gates, where a board announced, as Drina remembered, that this was a residential ballet school.

The drive was winding and climbed quite steeply. It was bordered with masses of bright yellow flowers with big green ruffs and Drina thought vaguely that Jenny would have known their names.

Mrs Chester glanced at her watch.

"A quarter past twelve. You're in nice time for lunch. And mind you try to eat a good meal, Drina. You ate scarcely any breakfast."

"Yes, Granny," Drina said meekly, though she was sure that food would choke her. Very probably her grandmother knew that, but, always a practical person, it was one of her most characteristic remarks. Drina was suddenly not in the least deceived by the usual brisk manner – her grandmother was suffering nearly as much, or perhaps more, than she was herself.

When the Manor came in sight it was a big place, built of warm old brick. It had several gables and twisted Tudor chimneys. Not far away, to the right, rather surprisingly, was a very ancient-looking brick-and-flint church with a squat tower.

"Village churches are often in the grounds of manor houses," said Mrs Chester. "As at Great Hampden." Then she leaned forward to speak to the driver, as the taxi drew up on the gravel before the front door. "Will you wait for me, please? I want to catch the next train back to London. Just before one, I believe. I shan't be many minutes."

It was then that panic took possession of Drina. She told herself frantically that she was thirteen and a half, that she had acted in a real play and not been afraid of a West End audience, that heaps of girls had been at boarding-school for years when they were her age and apparently coped with it perfectly well and even enjoyed it. And this was no ordinary boarding-school – it was a ballet school.

The fact remained that she would have liked to bolt like a rabbit; anything not to have to be left alone in a strange community, where there would be no escape home at four o'clock.

The door was opened by a young girl, who looked very foreign. She smiled in a friendly way.

"Oh, yes, Madame. Mrs Chester? Miss Sutherland expect you. This way, please. The luggage I will see to."

They followed the girl through the large, oak-panelled hall and down several corridors to a big, panelled sitting-room. They had not waited more than two minutes when Miss Sutherland, the headmistress, came in. She was a tall woman, with reddish hair; not in the least like small, quiet, grey-haired Miss Lane.

"So this is your granddaughter, Mrs Chester? How do you do, my dear? I hope you'll be very happy with us. It'll be a great change at first, no doubt, but everyone seems happy here."

"I'm afraid my taxi is waiting," said Mrs Chester and Drina gave her an agonised glance.

"Oh, yes, of course. And you saw over the school when you were here before. Then perhaps Drina would like to go to the front door with you and then I'll show her to her bedroom myself. The girls are all upstairs, getting tidy for lunch, which we have at twelve-thirty."

So that was that, and in a very short time Drina was standing on the step, watching the taxi disappearing round the first curve of the drive. When she turned back into the hall she found Miss Sutherland examining, or pretending to examine, a large noticeboard, and the headmistress turned after a moment to give her an understanding glance.

"Come along upstairs. I believe that your trunk has arrived and your other things have been taken up. Matron will help you to unpack this afternoon. You'll feel strange at first, especially arriving so late in the term, but I've heard very good reports of you from the Dominick and, as a matter of fact, I saw your performance in *Argument in Paris*. I thought you were very good. It was a pity the play didn't run."

Drina smiled back, though her face felt stiff. "Everyone was sorry. But I want to be a dancer, not an actress."

"Well, we'd better hurry or the bell will be going. You'll want to take off your outdoor clothes and wash your hands."

Drina followed her up the curving main staircase. The house was beautiful and obviously very old, and there were low bowls of the golden flowers with green ruffs on tables in the hall and in the upper corridor. Everywhere smelt warm and there was the fragrance of polish. Cheerful voices sounded in the distance and someone was humming the Mazurka from *Les Sylphides*. Through a big window halfway along the corridor was a view over the beechwoods and the wide valley to the hills beyond. It seemed a poor exchange for Drina's glimpse of Lambeth Bridge and the river from her own little room.

Miss Sutherland paused outside a door labelled "Ivory". Drina saw the name with a sense of shock. Even after more than a year she could still not always believe that her mother had been one of the greatest dancers of all time.

"We call most of the bedrooms and dormitories after famous dancers. The students like it much better than numbers. You're in a room for six." And she opened the door briskly, revealing the room's five occupants combing hair, washing at the two fitted basins in a corner, or merely gossiping.

They all spun round, apparently startled to see the headmistress herself.

4

First Days at Chalk Green

"This is the new girl, Drina Adams. Drina, these are Hildegarde Hermann from Germany, Emilia Riante, who comes from Italy, Joan and Sue Meredith, and Christine Gifford. They're all about your age. Girls, you'll look after Drina and bring her down to lunch when the bell rings? I'll tell Matron that you've arrived, Drina." And she was gone.

Drina was left facing the five curious pairs of eyes and for a moment there was rather a blank silence. Then Hildegarde, a brown-haired girl whose smooth locks were held back in a tidy ponytail, smiled and said in clear but slightly stilted English:

"How do you do, Drina? Your bed is there, beside Joan's. Your trunk, you see, and also your case."

"It's the bed that squeaks!" said one of the Merediths and giggled in a friendly enough way. She and her sister were twins and so alike that Drina, looking at them, felt more bewildered than ever.

"Thank you," Drina said and moved over to the squeaky bed, unfastening her coat as she went. She had never read many school stories, but she did feel uncommonly like the heroine of one. After all the suffering of the past week it was almost too much, this contact with five strange girls. She was not normally shy and she had learned to get on easily enough with people after her years at the Selswick School and the Dominick, but now she couldn't think of anything at all to say.

"I suppose you *are* English?" asked the very good-looking girl called Christine. Her voice was clear and decisive and she looked extremely assured and a good deal more critical than the rest. She reminded Drina immediately and rather uncomfortably of Queenie Rothington.

"Of course she is, with a name like Adams!" said one of the twins quickly.

"Well, she doesn't look it, and whoever heard of anyone English called Drina?"

"I'm partly Italian," Drina said, as she took her comb from her shoulder-bag and ran it quickly through her shining dark hair. "But I've never been to Italy." Her real name was Andrina Adamo, but she was not going to tell them that. For one thing her grandmother preferred her to be called Adams, and for another she had vowed to herself never to use the name again until she was ready to tell everyone that her mother had been the great dancer Elizabeth Ivory. Quite a number of people might remember that Ivory had been married to a businessman from Milan called Andrea Adamo.

"I will tell you about Italy," said the very small girl called Emilia. "I am from Genoa. And so——"

A bell shrilled through the house and at the same moment one of the twins said "Bronwen Jones told us that you're the girl who was in the play, *Argument in Paris*. How wonderful to be in a real play! She said you were the little ballet dancer, Françoise."

"It didn't run," said Christine.

Drina washed her hands hastily, looking at them as she wiped them. Four faces were friendly and curious; the fifth was definitely not so friendly.

"No," she said to Christine, "it didn't run." She knew that Queenie, and probably Christine herself, would have lost no time in pointing out that the little dancer, Françoise, had had almost universally good notices in the newspapers.

Christine shrugged and laughed. "Oh, well, come on. I'm starving! What do a few weeks in a play matter, anyway?" She tossed her bright hair and marched from the room.

"Her mother was with the Dominick Company for a time," said Hildegarde as they all followed. "And also with the Royal Ballet. She was Lois Leedon. Her most favourite role was in *Coppélia*."

"And aren't we tired of hearing about it?" said one twin, *sotto voce*.

For one wild moment Drina yearned to say as loudly as possible, "And my mother was Ivory!" Many and many a time, especially when Queenie boasted that her mother was a ballerina called Beryl Bertram, she had been most sorely tempted. But she had made her vow and that was the end of it.

Girls were pouring down a flight of side stairs and when they reached the lower corridor there were boys, too, though not nearly so many of them. The noise was considerable; evidently there was no rule of silence at Chalk Green Manor. The dining-room was very large and panelled like most of the house. The tables were quite small, mostly seating five or six, and there were flowers and catkins on each one. A thin, elderly woman in a white coat and head-dress came up to Drina as she hesitated.

"You're Drina Adams? How do you do, my dear? Yes, sit there with the rest of Ivory, though you'll find you don't have to stick to the same table all the time. Come up to your room after lunch and we'll deal with your unpacking. There's a 'character' class at half past one, but you won't want to go today."

Drina sat down, aware that several boys and girls had gone to a hatch at one side. Emilia came back with two plates of soup and put one down in front of the new girl.

"Very good soup. Here the food is very nice."

Drina made an effort to swallow a few mouthfuls, but the tightness in her throat made it very difficult. She looked about her at the chattering groups; at the adults at what seemed to be the staff tables near one of the big windows. Incredulity swept over her in a wave. It had all happened so quickly, so frighteningly quickly. Last week she had been happy at the Dominick; now she was at a ballet boarding-school and she felt utterly miserable and homesick; cut off from everyone and everything.

"I don't know how I shall bear it!" she thought.

At the end of the meal, when everyone was beginning to disperse, Drina felt a tug at her sleeve and turned to find a younger girl at her elbow. Drina was small for her age, but she was, even so, almost a head taller than the bright-faced eleven-year-old, with the high cheekbones and rather long, dark-brown hair.

"You're Drina Adams, aren't you? Jan, my cousin, wrote to me. And Matron says she's just remembered something she has to do, so she won't be able to help you to unpack until after half past one. Would you like me to show you round?"

Her voice was slightly singsong and very attractive,

and, as Drina hesitated, she added cheerfully:

"What a silly I am! I'm Bronwen Jones. I'm Welsh. Would you like to see round?"

"It's awfully nice of you," said Drina.

"Unless you'd rather have one of the older ones? But I'm *quite* an old inhabitant. I came when I was nine and a half. That's more than six terms ago."

"No, I'd like you to." Drina could not hurt her feelings, though all she really wanted was to escape for a time.

"Jan said you felt really bad over leaving the Dominick," Bronwen said as she led her charge along the corridor. "But this is *part* of the Dominick, of course."

"But it's so cut off! All these woods, and – and – I can't feel it's the same," Drina burst out.

Bronwen gave her a shrewd, friendly look.

"Don't you like the country? We all love it. We have a splendid time, especially in summer. There's even a swimming pool."

"I don't *know* the country. Not properly. It's even almost a year since I stayed at the farm in Warwickshire where I sometimes go."

Bronwen stopped to poke some of the golden flowers into place. "These are winter aconites. Did you know? They're almost over now, but there were lots in the woods as well as along the drive. We go walking and cycling. The hills are lovely – so lonely. Not high like the mountains at home, but sort of secret." She opened a door that led to what seemed to be a covered passage. "The studios and practice rooms are all in the new building at the back. Oh, indeed you will like it. Jan says you will, quite soon."

Jan, thought Drina, with unaccustomed sourness,

knew far more than she did herself, then. But she could not help cheering up a trifle when she saw the extremely light and modern studios, the small theatre, and the little room that housed the school's splendid record library. Bronwen's thin brown fingers waved excitedly at the cabinets that held the records.

"We've got all the ballet recordings. Sometimes we have concerts. Yesterday evening we had *Les Sylphides*, and some of *Giselle*, and the *Emperor Concerto* and the *Clock Symphony* as well. Miss Church – she's the music teacher – says we mustn't only listen to ballet music. And the *Emperor* is splendid, don't you think? It makes me go hot with excitement towards the end. Miss Lerrigano is ballet mistress. Your ballet teacher will be Miss O'Donnell; she's really nice. And your class teacher is Miss Crawford. She's quite nice, too, but rather a scaring sort of person sometimes. She takes us for English and history, so I know. And a week on Saturday we're going to London to see the Dominick Company. It's *Giselle* and *Gaité Parisienne*. Miss Lerrigano doesn't care for *Gaité Parisienne*. She says it's rather a bad ballet. But the next Saturday is getting too near the end of term." She stopped, breathless, leaving Drina for a moment faintly comforted. At least that would be something to look forward to during the coming days. Even a glimpse of London, even two or three hours in the Dominick Theatre, would be a help.

Her indefatigable guide rushed her back into the house and displayed classrooms and common rooms, the library and the art room with enormous pride.

"Isn't it a lovely house? Until we came six years ago it belonged to a very ancient family, but they hadn't the money to keep it up. There isn't time to show you the church, but you can see all the Grandown memorials there. There's a beautiful Tudor one, with six daughters behind their mother and six sons behind their father and two little ones by themselves who died in infancy. Isn't that sad? They all have stone ruffs and such interesting faces."

By now Drina was more bewildered than ever and, though she could not help liking Bronwen, she began to long to get away from her. It was a relief when the other girl gave a cry of surprise.

"It's later than I thought! I've got a class. Can you find your way to Ivory?"

"I expect so." And Drina thanked her and found the side stairs, meeting the twins and Christine on their way down wearing practice costume and shoes.

"Matey's waiting for you!" the twins said in chorus and dashed ahead of Christine, their fingers linked.

Matron tackled the unpacking briskly, showing Drina which sections of the big cupboards were hers.

"All your dancing things in here – that's right. Shoes in that cubby-hole, except for your walking shoes and those go downstairs in the cloakrooms. And your blouses there. What's the matter, my dear? Do you feel sick?"

Drina did indeed feel sick. The strain of the past few days was telling on her and she had eaten scarcely anything since the previous evening, but she shook her head and said as firmly as she could, "No, thank you."

Matron gave her a shrewd look, for Drina's health report had mentioned that she was exceptionally sensitive and highly strung, but she merely said:

"Well, perhaps a walk will do you good. Some of the girls are going to the farm with Miss Crawford and then to collect fresh catkins and buds for the hall and dining-room. Why don't you stay here quietly and read one of those beautiful new ballet books you've brought with you? I'll ask someone to collect you when they're ready."

Drina was glad of the momentary peace, but for once the ballet books held no solace. It was almost a relief when she found herself walking past the church and by a path through the woods with Miss Crawford and a group of rather younger girls. Only Emilia was there from Ivory and she was friendly enough, but seemed to realise that Drina preferred not to talk. The farm, with its brick-and-flint buildings and russet roof, seemed somehow to have grown out of that landscape. The chalky fields rolled behind it to more woods and a plough drawn by a scarlet tractor was turning up the almost colourless earth. The wind was very cold and the smell of earth and animals reminded Drina suddenly and sharply of Jenny. She would have given almost anything to be with her friend, savouring her calm commonsense.

Later they cut birch and hazel catkins in a climbing lane that Miss Crawford told the unresponsive new girl was part of the Icknield Way, and there was delight when someone found some sycamore buds quite well out. But the endless beech trees were not showing any green and the brooding woods seemed to Drina even more strange than they had been in summer.

"Aren't you glad to be out of town?" someone asked her cheerfully, scrambling down a muddy bank, and before she could stop herself Drina had cried "I *hate* the country!"

Everyone stared and someone giggled, and Drina flushed deeply. She had not meant to say that, even though it was the truth. But she felt "all wrong" and didn't really care in the least what they thought. Miss

Crawford said quietly:

"It must be a great change for you, Drina." And they all tramped on, not seeming to notice the cold. Drina would not have noticed it herself if she had been walking along the Embankment towards Westminster, but misery and lack of food had lowered her resistance.

Afterwards there was tea and then prep, during which Drina was given books and a timetable by Miss Crawford. Supper was just hot milk and buttered biscuits and at last it was bedtime. It had been the longest day that Drina ever remembered and she was deeply thankful when the lights were out and everyone had stopped whispering and giggling. But the wind in the trees kept her awake for a long time, as well as the strangeness of sharing a room with five other people. When at last she fell asleep she dreamed of being lost in the seemingly endless woodland.

Next morning at nine o'clock there was a ballet class and it was comforting to be at the *barre* again. The familiar movements, the familiar rhythms, made her feel more real at once, but her body felt rather stiff and she knew that she was not as good as usual. Miss O'Donnell corrected her more than once, but in quite a kindly way. It was no consolation to Drina, though, to hear Christine mutter, "Françoise isn't so specially good, is she?"

She knew quite well that she was not going to like Christine at all.

By lunchtime Drina had at last sorted out quite a number of people and various things were clear. That Christine had an excellent opinion of herself, and that the members of the staff seemed to like her but the girls not. That Emilia was homesick for Italy and loved to talk about her native city of Genoa. That Hildegarde was slow at lessons, even though she spoke and read English so well, but that she was a promising dancer, and that the twins, Joan and Sue, were like one person, unhappy if separated at all.

Emilia and Hildegarde might become her friends, even though just then she felt quite unable to cope with personal relationships, but the twins would never bother to grow very friendly with anyone else. And Christine, if she had real friends at all, looked for them amongst the slightly older girls – there was no one older than fifteen at Chalk Green – and amongst the boys.

Christine knew that Drina was miserable and seemed to take a pleasure in making irritating remarks.

I suppose all schools have a few girls who really aren't nice, Drina wrote to Jenny. *And I know you say that being ambitious brings out the worst in people. Christine, just like Queenie, thinks that she will be a great dancer one day, but then we all want to be good dancers one day. She seems to dislike me because I was in* Argument, *but perhaps it's because I'm not really very nice to know at the moment. But the others don't seem to care for her much.*

Oh, Jenny, I feel such an exile! I can hardly bear to hear Big Ben on the radio. I miss the Dominick so much, and coming out at four o'clock and seeing the Company sometimes, that I could die, if dying were so easy.

I wish you were here to lecture me. I'm sunk into self-pity and I keep on hating myself, but I can't stop. I thought I had more character; Miss Whiteway would be so ashamed of me if she knew. But she's terribly busy just now, because she's going away soon, and I can't write miserable letters to her.

I'm dancing badly, however hard I try, and I'm sure everyone wonders how I ever got that part in Argument.

The country is very muddy and very cold. I don't know how you like it so much. This afternoon we walked along the top of the ridge and there was a huge view – all the way across the plain, with villages here and there but not a soul anywhere in sight. And I couldn't believe that London is less than forty miles away. This place is like the end of the world, though the others seem to love it. They're getting quite excited because there will soon be primroses and violets and other things. You'll sympathise. Oh, do write to me as often as possible.

There came a day, when she had been at Chalk Green for nearly a week – seven interminable days – when Drina showed Christine that she had a temper. It was the day that her grandparents sailed for Australia and Drina's mind had been a good deal on that during the morning ballet class and lessons. She was rather behind the others when she went upstairs to wash and tidy herself for lunch.

Christine was inquisitive and rather over-interested in other people's possessions, and Drina arrived in time to find her poking her long fingers into the writing-case that had been her grandmother's present on her thirteenth birthday. It would not, perhaps, have mattered so much had Drina not hidden away in a back pocket several photographs of her mother – Elizabeth Ivory as Josette in *The Breton Wedding*, as Giselle, and as a young child: the latter was Drina's one treasured picture of Betsy Chester in the days when she was at the Dominick School.

The writing-case had a key and ordinarily Drina kept it locked, but she must have forgotten, for Christine was already groping into that very pocket.

In a flash Drina was across the room, her dark eyes blazing, her hair streaming back from her angry face.

"How dare you? How *dare* you? Put it down at once and if I catch you touching my private things again I'll *kill* you!"

Christine dropped the writing-case on the bed, and the others who had not, until then, noticed what she was doing gave cries of indignation.

"Oh, Christine!"

Drina was still clutching Christine's arm in a strong grip and the other girl shook herself free, alarmed, though she would never have admitted it, by the storm that had blown up.

"You horrible little spitfire! Who'd have thought you'd got such a temper! I wasn't doing any harm, only you always look as though you've got a secret in there."

"But even if she has——" Sue said. "It was awfully wrong of you Christine. We never thought——"

"In future," said Drina, coldly and clearly, "you'll leave my things alone. Or——or——"

"Oh, all right." And Christine laughed carelessly and went to wash her hands. "What a fuss about nothing! Drina, you did look as though you could kill me. I'm not sure that I oughtn't to tell Matron. You aren't safe."

"No, I'm not!" said Drina, her eyes still very bright. "But I shouldn't tell Matron if I were you. I've got Italian blood, don't forget." She was suddenly almost enjoying herself.

"There is the bell," said Hildegarde peaceably.

Drina locked her writing-case, combed her hair and flew after the others. She was ashamed of her outburst, but for the first time for many days she felt alive. Christine now knew that her things were to be respected and that was something.

5

The Meeting in the Wood

After lunch the twins found Drina, walking, as they nearly always did, with linked fingers. Even after a week Drina felt that she had no hope of telling them apart; they were alike in every detail.

"To the last hair and whisper," as one of the boys had said in Drina's hearing.

She was by no means the only one who was hopelessly puzzled by the Merediths. The problem was presumably going to be when they were old enough to be in the Company, something that seemed very likely to happen, as they were most promising dancers.

"You can't both dance Giselle on the same night!" Christine had said irritably, soon after Drina's arrival, for she, too, was never sure which was Sue and which Joan.

Now the twins advanced on Drina, smiling in so exactly the same way that it was positively uncanny and made her feel as though she were seeing double.

"I say! We're sorry that Christine was such a beast," one twin said. "We honestly hadn't noticed what she was doing, or of course we'd have stopped her."

"It's all right," said Drina. "It was awful of me to lose my temper like that. I don't often, and I always feel ashamed afterwards. But she's so like a girl called Queenie Rothington at the Dominick. I went for *her* once, and Igor Dominick heard every word."

Their blue eyes were very wide.

"The great man himself? How terrible for you! But Christine really is the end. We do wish she wasn't in Ivory, but we don't suppose we'll ever get rid of her."

"I suppose there's always *someone* like her," remarked Drina, voicing her innermost thoughts. "Wherever you go, I mean."

"Oh, of course, and she's not absolutely the only one here, but we could be really happy in Ivory without her. Except," and that particular twin hesitated tactfully, "that *you* aren't very happy, anyway. You do rather hate it, don't you?"

Drina looked at their identical, sympathetic faces and felt ashamed. "Yes, I do rather, but I know I shouldn't when you all love it and most of you are so nice. But it's not a bit like the Dominick. It's like – like being in a convent."

"What? With boys?" They giggled.

"Well, I suppose not. But at the Dominick something's always happening and we see Mr Dominick and Marianne Volonaise about the place. And the members of the Company are often next door. We never speak to them, but we see Catherine Colby and Peter Bernoise going to their cars. I miss it all dreadfully."

"Well, we're going to London on Saturday," they said. "You'll like that, won't you?"

And Drina did, in fact, find herself living for the time when she would be in the Dominick Theatre again. The days seemed to pass very slowly, once the ballet class was over, and even that was not the pleasure it should have been. She was not dancing well and, though she tried desperately, her old ease and smoothness would not come. Astonishingly and disturbingly her well-trained body did not always obey her. Her *port de bras* were stiff and awkward, when usually they earned her the most praise.

However, Saturday morning did dawn at last and, after a particularly early lunch, the whole school was packed into private buses. They sped away towards High Wycombe and very soon, as the woods and hills began to fall behind, Drina felt happier. London lay ahead and the smell and atmosphere of a real theatre.

London looked even more colourless in the gloomy, cold weather than the countryside had done, but to Drina it was beautiful. The towers of Westminster, the grey river, the modern curves of Waterloo Bridge, the crowds and crowds of people: all gave her sharp pleasure. They were early at the theatre, but as they streamed into the Grand Circle Drina saw that there were a number of red and grey uniforms across the aisle. And then she saw Rose's smiling, eager face and her waving hand.

"Oh, please! Please!" she cried to Miss O'Donnell, who had never seen her so animated. "May I go and speak to my friend Rose?"

Rose was with Jan, Jill and Betty. There was no sign of Daphne and Queenie, as Drina saw with relief. She noticed, with a faint sense of shock, how very pale Rose looked in the bright lights of the theatre, and she seemed thinner, too.

They all greeted Drina rather as though she were a being from another world, which was indeed just how Drina felt herself. If she had just stepped off a flying saucer she could not have felt very different.

"It's so lovely to see you all!" she cried, plumping herself down in an as yet unoccupied seat behind them. "It seems like years!"

"So it does," Rose said sadly. "I've missed you dreadfully. Tell us how you've been getting on."

"I'd sooner hear *your* news."

"Oh, there's nothing much," Betty said. "Mr Dominick sprained his ankle and has been hobbling round on a stick. Madam" – she meant Marianne Volonaise – "gave the Juniors a terrific lecture about manners and deportment. You know, walking quietly in the street and not chewing gum. Some of them have got into a dreadful habit of chewing. She says that prospective ballet dancers should always try to look elegant and attractive. The girls, that is. The boys have teased us horribly and kept on saying, 'That isn't elegant!' But *they* got a lecture, too. Some of them had been fighting in the Square."

"And Mr Amberdown watched some of the ballet classes yesterday with Madam. It was really most unnerving."

"Yes, it must have been," Drina said wistfully. She would gladly have been unnerved to see Colin Amberdown, the ballet critic, again. It was he who had told her that her mother was Ivory, and who therefore knew all about her secret.

"But tell us – they *do* look a stuffy lot! Are they as good as they look? *Do* you hate it? Rose says you do."

"I do rather, though I'm trying really hard to settle down. I don't like the country a bit and the weather's been awful since I went to Chalk Green – such a lot of rain and cold winds. Most of them don't seem to mind. They love the woods and Bledlow Ridge."

"Tell us their names."

Drina glanced across the aisle at her Chalk Green contemporaries. "That very striking girl with the bright hair is Christine Gifford. I don't like her at all. She's inquisitive and says horrid things. I caught her poking into my writing-case and I said I'd kill her. I shocked everyone, I think, and I was even shocked myself. I *could* have killed her!"

"Goodness! And the twins? They're as alike as two peas. We've often seen them."

"I still don't know them apart and no one else does, really. They're nice, but very – very self-absorbed. They come from Cheshire and seem awfully well off. They have lovely things. That girl with the brown ponytail is German. She's from Freiburg in the Black Forest and she's nearly always good-tempered and kind. I like her. And the one beside her, Emilia, is Italian. I thought I might some time ask her to teach me some Italian. Granny said I might go there, perhaps this year, but now it'll be next year, I suppose." And Drina sighed.

"Do you like the boys?"

"Oh, yes. They're all right. They don't have a lot to do with us and some of them are very young. They have their own common rooms and ballet classes. There's a French boy called Jacques who's good fun, and even a Russian. But I'm afraid I haven't really tried to make friends with anyone."

Rose gave her an understanding look, for she had received more than one decidedly gloomy letter.

"It is a shame. And we do miss you. But perhaps your grandparents will come home sooner than you think."

"It can't be *too* soon," Drina confessed. "But I'm afraid it will be after Christmas. It seems a lifetime away!"

Then she had to go back to her seat, and soon everyone was settled and that lovely, satisfying moment came when the house lights went out and the curtain softly rose to the familiar *Giselle* music.

Immediately Drina forgot all her troubles. Catherine Colby was dancing Giselle and her dancing was always a delight. As the simple peasant girl in love she was so airy and happy, with just the right appealing charm. The cool, woody smell of the stage came up to Drina's nostrils, but she only noticed it subconsciously. She was lost in pleasure as the act went on and the royal hunting party arrived in their gorgeous clothes. The music seemed to strike her right to the heart, especially that haunting tune that belonged so much to Giselle herself.

The moment of betrayal, when Giselle understood that her lover had deceived her, took Drina forward in her seat and she remained there, tensely, until the end of the act when Giselle lay dead with everyone grouped about her.

The second act of *Giselle* was one of the first ballets she had ever seen, in the shabby old Grand Theatre in Willerbury. Then she had been enchanted, but it had been an enchantment without knowledge. Now she knew the meaning of each lovely movement and was held spellbound, not only because of the total effect of the setting, the music and the movement, but because she knew how very good the Dominick *corps de ballet* was. Every critic had said that the dancers were at the top of their form this season, and it was true. Watching their white-clad figures, Drina thought passionately that she would be content if she could only find herself a member of the Company, a Wili. Of course it was an impossible dream that she might ever dance Giselle, but that didn't really matter.

Suddenly, as Albrecht danced on and on at the bidding of the merciless Wilis, she was visited by a deep sadness: a deep dissatisfaction with herself. The ballet was so lovely that it made her realise sharply just how "all wrong" she had been since her grandparents had broken the news about Chalk Green Manor.

"I will try to be better," Drina thought, but when, after tea in the Strand, they were in the buses again, speeding back to Buckinghamshire, she felt the familiar depression. Tomorrow was Sunday. That meant morning church in the ancient building near the Manor, where a few village people and occasionally odd visitors joined them. Then letter writing and a walk in the cold and muddy woods.

And it might have meant the Tate Gallery with Rose, or Hampstead Heath if the weather were fine enough, with muffins afterwards for tea!

It was suddenly April and the cold, dreary spring at last decided to improve. The sun poured into Chalk Green Manor and they practised at the *barre* in a blaze of light. It was no longer so chilly in the bedrooms and getting up in the morning was much more pleasant. Most of the pupils went for a short run before breakfast, and up till then Drina had avoided any such exercise. But the sunshine made a good deal of difference and she found herself willing enough to dash down the drive with Hildegarde and Emilia.

She began, almost without noticing it, to feel more cheerful, but was still worried because her dancing was not up to standard and the harder she tried the worse it seemed to be.

"You're so very tense," said Miss O'Donnell. "What *is* the matter, Drina?" But Drina couldn't tell her that she had felt tense for weeks now and didn't know how to undo the trouble.

In a very few days they would be breaking up for the Easter holidays and it was a relief to think of Jenny.

Marianne Volonaise paid fairly frequent visits to Chalk Green, which came under her ultimate jurisdiction in the same way as the Dominick School in London. Her visits always caused a stir and she had been at least five times since Drina's arrival at the Manor. But she only saw the great Miss Volonaise in the distance and certainly never expected to speak to her. Still, it was nice to see her slim, elegant figure about the place: a link with London and the ballet world.

"Madam *again*!" said one of the twins on the last Monday of term when they spied a familiar black car outside the front door. "I hope she doesn't watch the 'character' class this afternoon. Last time she did Joan was so nervous that she slipped and sat down in the very middle of a dance."

"I thought it was Sue," said Christine, rather crossly. The twins' similarity to each other always irritated her.

"No, Joan," said both, smiling with perfect good temper. "But we neither of us want to do it again."

Miss Volonaise did not appear at the afternoon classes and Drina thought very little about her. She did not even notice whether or not the black car was still there, for she left the house by the side door at half past three.

The students of Chalk Green Manor were fairly free to take their outdoor exercise how they pleased. If they wished they could join cycling or walking parties, or even riding ones, for there were some keen riders at the Manor. But, if they preferred it, the ones over twelve could go where they liked in small parties of their own choice. Provided they behaved sensibly and were back in good time for tea at five, no one minded. But they were not supposed to go out of the grounds quite alone, except to the village of Chalk Green where one of the cottages housed a tiny post office and sweet shop.

The grounds, however, were large, and in no real sense "grounds" at all. There was a rose garden and an orchard and a paddock where the riders kept their ponies, but for the most part there were woods near the house. A still, dark larchwood climbed up the slopes of the ridge and the great beechwoods stretched to east and west. The Chalk Green estate still included the farm and several fields, but the "grounds" were taken to be the nearer woods.

At first, of course, the woodland had oppressed Drina, but somehow the trees seemed different during the dazzling April afternoon, with cuckoos calling from across the valley, and a carpet of violets, primroses, wood sorrel and wood anemones underfoot. The beech trees were in bud and here and there was a branch bright with unfurling leaves. The smooth grey trunks stretched away into the distance and sometimes there were grey squirrels flying up them, pausing on a branch to look down with sharp, curious eyes.

So Drina escaped from her contemporaries on that particular Monday afternoon and ran away into the nearer woods. It was good to be alone, for solitariness was not easy to enjoy at boarding-school.

She swished her way through the deep masses of old beech leaves, stopping occasionally to look at a flower. The others seemed to know the names of them all and the twins had said only the previous evening that chalk

country was wonderful for wild flowers. Orchids, they had said, of all sorts, thyme, rock roses, scabious, poppies, milkwort. Drina must see them all in summer.

For the first time, as she paused to gather a little bunch of violets to tuck into her blouse, she thought that she might like that. For the first time, too, she felt a sense of real well-being. The sun slanting through the beech trunks, the distant sound of cuckoos and wood pigeons, the crisp crackle of the old leaves under foot . . . And the wood was almost like a cathedral, so big and high.

She did what she had done only twice before in her life: found a patch of smooth grass at the edge of the wood, kicked off her shoes, flung off her grey jacket and began to dance. She had done it on the cliffs of Porth-din-Lleyn, and once on Romney Marsh under the vast sky, and each time she had felt truly happy. It was the same now. She danced with abandonment. No longer stiff and tense, but alive and warm, revelling in the spring sunlight and the spring smells . . . thinking of summer.

Then, at last, she realised that she was not alone. Someone wearing a dark red suit was standing at a little distance, watching her. It was Marianne Volonaise herself, quite alone and motionless.

Drina stopped dancing at once and groped for her shoes and jacket. Her face felt hot and she scarcely knew what to say. But perhaps there was no need to say anything. Madam probably didn't even know her name and wouldn't want to bother with a Junior.

But Marianne Volonaise did know her name. She called imperiously "Don't go away, please, Drina! I want to speak to you."

Carrying her jacket, her face still flushed above her emerald green blouse, Drina went slowly forward.

6

Back at the
Selswick School

As they faced each other Drina thought fleetingly that it was strange to see Madam in the country, hatless and holding a bunch of primroses. Always she had seemed so completely a city person: elegant, sophisticated, never a hair out of place. She really was a remote being, and a slightly feared one.

"That was a very charming dance," said Marianne Volonaise. "Did you make it up on the spur of the moment?"

Drina went pinker than ever. "Yes, Madam. I – I suddenly liked the wood. I think it was a Spring Dance."

"A future choreographer!" said Miss Volonaise, almost to herself. And then: "But you'd prefer to be a future ballerina?"

"I want to dance," Drina got out with some difficulty. "But some day I'd like to make dances, too. There have to be new ballets, don't there?"

"Certainly there do, or ballet would become a hopelessly static art. I was looking for you, my child. I saw you leave the house, but lost you for a time in the wood."

Drina gulped, for Madam's tone was grave. There

seemed no answer and she remained silent.

"I haven't heard a very good report of you since you transferred to Chalk Green. At first I didn't think it important, as we all knew you'd had a shock, being moved so hurriedly. But it can't go on, you know. You're capable of excellent school work, and of far better dancing than you've apparently been doing lately. Don't you like Chalk Green? Most people seem very happy here."

Her eyes were kind and quite obviously she was going to wait until she heard the truth, so Drina said honestly, "I haven't liked it. But I *have* tried, truly. I've kept on hating myself, but then the more I tried to work the worse I seemed to get. It – it seemed so awful to be in exile."

"Exile? You think of it like that?"

"Anyone would, after the Dominick!" Drina burst out. "I loved the Dominick. I was so wonderfully happy. And being in London, seeing everyone, knowing what was going on. I don't like the country much, and——"

"You liked it enough just now to make a Spring Dance!"

"Yes. Suddenly it was different, or *I* was different. It's such a lovely day. I hated the mud and the cold wind, and the woods seemed frightening before."

The woman who had always seemed as though she belonged entirely to cities seated herself suddenly on a fallen tree trunk and patted the smooth grey wood beside her.

"Sit down. But put on your jacket. I don't want you to get cold. Now, look, Drina, we thought you had both character and personality, but you haven't been showing much character lately, have you?"

"I did *try*."

"I'm sure you did, and I know it was hard for you. Perhaps your grandmother wasn't very wise to give you so little a warning, but she told me that she didn't want to divulge her plans until everything was settled. Some people are like that." And she smiled. "You had enough strength of character to come back to the Dominick with a smile when *Argument in Paris* finished so suddenly and to get on with your work as though nothing had happened. That was a big test, for you'd tasted the pleasure of a certain amount of success and public acclaim. *This* is far harder, because you find it dull at Chalk Green and you feel cut off from your family and your old friends. But you *can* settle down here and be happy. I believe you've started already."

Drina was looking down, fighting for composure. The sympathetic voice made her feel much less alone than she had done. It surprised and moved her to realise that the great ones – Miss Volonaise herself and perhaps even Igor Dominick – knew of her troubles.

"I think – perhaps I have. But I've felt so tight——"

"You'll loosen up if you stop thinking about it. You weren't 'tight' just now. Don't worry at all, but have good holidays and come back with a cheerful face next term. What are your hobbies – interests?"

This time Drina looked up. "Oh, well, ballet, Madam. It's my – everything."

A long, perfectly manicured hand came out and took Drina's slightly grubby fingers.

"My dear child! That's all very well. A dancer does have to think and breathe dancing and the life of a ballet dancer doesn't leave a great deal of time for other interests. And yet there *must* be other things, or that dancer will be a very narrow person and not a great artist. If you're narrow at thirteen you're likely to be just as narrow at twenty-three or thirty-three. What about reading?"

"B-ballet books, mostly. Not silly stories, but b-books about heaps of aspects of it."

"Oh, well, try reading books about other countries for a change. Books about art, mountains, even books about the countryside. What about art? Have you got a favourite artist?"

Drina suddenly met her eyes, smiling in rather a shamefaced way.

"Degas."

"I might have known! Anyone else?"

"Well, I do love Van Gogh. All those heavenly colours – the house at Arles, and cornfields, and people with interesting faces. And I like Monet——"

"Better! Now see here! You've got a real chance to learn to know and love the country. Try and look at it intelligently and with wide-open eyes. It may be the only chance you'll ever have, for when your grandparents come home you'll return to London. When I was a child," said Miss Volonaise surprisingly, "I lived in the heart of Brittany. Not by the sea – inland. There was just a little village, where everyone was rather poor and the country was very stony and bare, with great standing-stones like the ones in Cornwall. There wasn't much to do, but I was happy. I loved to help in the fields and play in the river with the other children. That's a long, long time ago. When I was nearly eleven I got the chance to live in Paris with my grandparents and after that it was all dancing, all cities. But I'm glad I had that country childhood. Now I must get back! I'm due in London soon after half past five. Try to make the best of Chalk Green and perhaps, though it seems impossible now, you'll even be sorry to leave it when the time comes to go back to the Dominick."

They both rose and Drina stood looking at her.

"Yes – Miss Volonaise."

"You don't believe me? But I think it will grow on you. By the way, there's one piece of good news for you. Your friend, Rose Conway, is joining you here next term. That's partly why I came today – to fix it up."

Drina's eyes blazed. "Oh, but – I don't understand! Rose isn't a bit well off, and——"

"We've given her a scholarship on health grounds. She'll never stay the course in London and she's a very promising dancer. She needs a more balanced diet – though you needn't tell her so – and country air." Then she pressed Drina's rather bony shoulder and said, as she began to walk away, "The worst's over, I'm sure. Next term will be better."

Left alone in the wood, Drina sank down again on the tree trunk and stared blankly into space. Her cheeks burned and her heart beat rather quickly. It had been such a surprising conversation and never again would Marianne Volonaise seem so remote, even if they never had any more intimate conversations. Madam had been kind and warm and the fact that Drina was not forgotten was a great comfort.

The next morning there was a letter from Rose.

Oh, Drina, I'm coming to Chalk Green next term! Isn't it astonishing? I've been given a scholarship, and a grant for uniform and extras. It's because I'm anæmic or something and need country air. They told my mother that my dancing's very promising and Mum says she'll miss me, but

*it will be a wonderful chance to go to boarding-school. I
don't want to leave the Dominick, but it won't be so bad
when it means being with you.*

Just before the end of term Drina plucked up the
courage to go to Matron and ask if she could be in
Rose's dormitory next term, and Matron smiled and
said that she would do her best.

"But I don't promise, mind. The bedroom lists
always give me a very bad headache, but if she's your
friend it might be best. You'd both be happier."

So it was in quite a cheerful mood that Drina packed
all her things, especially as she had just had an air-
letter from her grandmother, saying that the long
voyage was doing them both good and her grandfather
was a different person already.

Even Christine was quite bearable during the last
hours at Chalk Green, for Drina was much too busy to
let her remarks bother her. Christine was going to Paris
for Easter and had bored everyone to distraction with
the constant retailing of her plans.

"Anyone would think that no one else was going
anywhere!" said one of the twins during the last
breakfast of the term. "We're going to Holland, but that
doesn't mean a thing."

"And Hildegarde's flying to Germany at two
o'clock!" agreed Drina, who was a trifle over-awed by
the unconcerned way the pupils of Chalk Green flew
about the world. Paris, certainly, was nothing at all,
when Emilia was flying to Milan that evening, and
three of the youngest students were flying all the way
to India the next day. But Christine continued all
through that last meal to expect attention. She was
going to the ballet at the *Opéra*. She was going to do
this and that.

"Pity she can't *stay* in Paris!" someone mumbled.

"She's just like Queenie Rothington at the Dominick," Drina sighed to Emilia.

After all these exciting plans Drina's own short journey to Willerbury seemed hardly worth mentioning. She was not going up to London, but was to travel to Oxford with Miss O'Donnell and several of the other pupils, and from there catch a train to Willerbury.

It was very exciting and satisfying to think of seeing Jenny again and the time passed quickly. From the train Drina watched the lambs capering in the fields and thought that slow streams and willow trees were the most typical things in that part of Oxfordshire. The hedges were astar with blackthorn and there were primroses and cowslips on the banks. Misery seemed far behind her, especially when Jenny came flying along the platform, her rosy face alight with pleasure.

"Drina! Oh, Drina! I *am* glad to see you! Your trunk arrived yesterday. Is there only your case and holdall? And the little radio? Mother's outside in the car."

Willerbury did not seem to have changed in the year since Drina had been away, except that there were some new buses, and the old Grand Theatre had been painted. A play was advertised.

"I hoped there might be some ballet!" said Drina as they were stopped by the traffic lights. Then she added, as Jenny laughed, "I had a talk with Miss Volonaise in the wood the other day and she said just the same sort of things that you do, Jenny. Not to get too absorbed in ballet and to have other interests."

"I'll help," Jenny vowed. "I've told you before that it's my mission in life to keep you down to earth. I do think you ought to learn to milk for a start!"

"Poor Drina!" cried Mrs Pilgrim, with a glance at the guest. "I'm sure she'd hate that. You don't alter much, Drina. You're still very small. A whole head shorter than Jenny."

"Oh, I'm going to be the fat woman at the fair," Jenny said cheerfully, and certainly she had grown even plumper than she had been at New Year. "My only hope is to grow tall as well, or I'll be as broad as I'm long! And by the way, Drina, I'm *not* starting the way I mean to go on. How would you like to go to the last class at the Selswick School tonight? I met Miss Selswick and told her you were coming and she said she'd love it if you'd go along and join in."

"Oh, yes!" Drina exclaimed, immediately thrilled. "Of course I'll go. But it's awfully sad. The last class!"

"Actually someone's bought the school, so it won't close down. Joy and Mark are really thrilled."

It was pleasant to be at Jenny's home again, settling down in the little room where she had once practised. The *barre* had gone now, since Jenny herself had no interest in dancing, and it was used as a guest room.

The boys were in for tea, all but Philip, who was a medical student in London and who was going walking in Scotland at Easter.

"Did he ever call and see you, Drina?" Jenny asked and Drina shook her head.

"No, and now he *can't*. It seems awful to think of strangers in the flat."

After tea Drina set off with Jenny for the Selswick School, carrying practice shoes and clothes in a little case lent by Jenny.

"I'm going to watch," Jenny announced. "And at the same time I shall thank my stars that I'm free of *port de bras* and *demi-pliés* in the second position! And afterwards we'll forget that such a thing as ballet exists."

It was very strange to walk through the door of the Selswick School again and Drina was thrilled because old Mr Hobbs, the caretaker, remembered her. He acted as doorkeeper during the hours that the school was open and had seemed part of her life in the old days.

It was fun to meet some of her old friends, particularly Joy Kelly and Mark Playford, and to go up to the studio with them, chattering all the time.

"You're awfully important now, aren't you?" Joy said. "After being at the Dominick for so long and having that part in a real London play."

And Drina laughed, shaking her head. How little they knew! She was just one of the crowd at Chalk Green and not even as good a dancer as some of her contemporaries.

Janetta Selswick greeted her very warmly.

"My dear Drina! How glad I am to see you again! I hear you're at Chalk Green now. It was quite a surprise. I'd thought I'd be seeing you, and perhaps even teaching you, at the Dominick. Though I'm mainly having senior students."

"She's in exile, Miss Selswick," said Jenny, the only one in ordinary clothes. "She hates it."

And Drina, blushing, said hastily, "It isn't really so bad. But nothing like the Dominick."

Drina enjoyed the class, for her tension seemed to have gone and she felt completely supple and sure of herself. She lost herself in the familiar movements and exercises and did not know that Janetta Selswick was watching her with deepest interest and pleasure. This was the ten-year-old girl who had watched in a corner by the piano one day and had later appeared with her grandmother, who had assured Madame that "Drina is to learn purely for pleasure. There is no question of her ever making dancing her career." And the girl had made the excuse of a lost handkerchief to fly back and blurt out that her grandmother hadn't quite got it right. *She* wanted to be a dancer and promised to work hard.

Janetta Selswick had no idea that Drina Adams was the daughter of a very great dancer. She had no idea that Elizabeth Ivory's own mascot was in the little case in the cloakroom, the mascot that had been left behind when the dancer set off on that tragic air journey to the United States, when the plane crashed into the sea and everyone was drowned. But she felt, looking at that absorbed pale face, the slim, trained body, that here was some important quality that none of the others possessed. Drina danced well, she had personality and looks, but there was something else as well.

"If ever a child was dedicated to an art she is," she thought and hoped most ardently that, in the years to come, Drina might have the chance. Though you could never be quite sure. Out of many hundreds of dancers, perhaps thousands, only one might have the makings of a ballerina. And thirteen was still much too early to tell.

"But I'd almost take a bet on it," she told herself.

At the end of the class the ballet pupils made a presentation to Miss Selswick and there were little speeches and smiles and some carefully concealed tears. Janetta herself was moved, for she had had her school for a long time and it was a wrench to give it up.

"If I'd been Madame I'd have cried my eyes out," said Drina as she and Jenny sat by the fire quite late that evening. "But I'm glad I was there. Oh, Jenny, this

is nice! Three whole weeks!"

"After Easter we're all going to the farm," Jenny told her. "Father and Mother and us, and two of the boys. Donny and Bill are going away with friends. And this time we won't let you catch cold. I still remember how terrible I felt when you were ill and couldn't go back to the Dominick for ages last year."

"Oh, I won't catch cold," said Drina casually. "I'm stronger now. And it will be nice to see the farm."

"Your kitten, Esmeralda, is a huge smoky cat. I told you ages ago it's a he and not a she, didn't I? He's a terrific mouser."

And Drina, shuddering, said she hoped that Esmeralda, out of love for his mistress, wouldn't make any gifts of mice!

"Sweet little things, with velvety backs and tiny paws!" said Jenny mischievously. "I sometimes wish that cats weren't such horrors, but you can't alter nature."

They talked all the time they were undressing and washing and afterwards Jenny sat on Drina's bed, swinging her feet and listening to Drina's account of all that had happened at Chalk Green.

"Never mind. You're with Jenny now. And if I had much of that Christine I'd wring her neck! You do seem to meet some awful people."

"And some nice ones, too," Drina said sleepily. "Oh, Jenny, how sane you seem and downright and comforting. Better than anyone else."

"I should hope so," said Jenny roundly, "when I'm your sort of sister." She made for the door.

"There'll be no rising-bell in the morning! Mother says you're to have your breakfast in bed as a special treat."

7

To the
Memorial Theatre

Within a very short time Chalk Green Manor seemed a dream. It was much more peaceful to sleep in the little room next to Jenny's than in Ivory with the twins, Hildegarde, Emilia and Christine. It was a pleasant change to have time to talk and potter about after breakfast, and even pleasant to help Mrs Pilgrim with the dusting or the washing up. Later Drina and Jenny did the shopping, Jenny carrying a blue bag and Drina a scarlet one, and they slipped back easily into their old, casual relationship where all jokes were understood and there was no need to hide sudden thoughts in case one or the other might be critical. They were very different in character and ambitions, but that seemed no handicap. As Jenny said, they might have been two sisters who got on exceptionally well together. It was restful, comfortable, and just what Drina needed.

In one thing Jenny had altered – she had at last grown out of liking Westerns. Drina was decidedly relieved to hear it, as she found Westerns very boring. Jenny's new taste ran to the better type of comedy and occasional murder and adventure stories.

"And of course one's about farming," she said. "But

there are so few of those. I did see one last week on television, but it was really stupid. That young farmer wouldn't have prospered in real life. He spent his whole time kissing his sweetheart and walking through the woods with her."

"But supposing *you* marry a farmer," Drina said, giggling. "Won't you want him to kiss you sometimes?"

"When he's done his work," Jenny said austerely, but her eyes were dancing. "What about that businessman from the provinces I said you'd marry?"

"That was just you being silly," Drina retorted with dignity. "I'm not going to marry until I'm at least thirty and then it will be someone to do with ballet."

"That's what *you* think!" said Jenny.

"It's what I intend," Drina insisted. "I shall have two daughters called Desda and Delphine."

"Oh, heavens!" Jenny cried. "You've planned a bit more than I knew. Are they to be dancers?"

"Oh, yes, of course. They'll go to the Dominick." Then Drina laughed and they went to wash their hands before lunch. She had simply invented Desda and Delphine on the spur of the moment.

Easter Monday Drina and Jenny spent with Joy Kelly at her home just outside Willerbury, and on the Tuesday they were all packed into the Pilgrims' big car and set off for the farm. The weather was brilliant but cold, the hawthorn hedges were very green and orchards were beginning to foam with blossom. Surprisingly Drina found that it was good to be back in the country. You scarcely got the feeling of spring in the streets of Willerbury and even the outskirts, where Jenny lived, were getting more built up every year. But in the green heart of Warwickshire it was truly April –

vivid and sweet-smelling and noisy with birdsong.

"I want to learn about the country," she said to Jenny. "The names of trees and flowers and birds. I never used to bother at all."

"You just about knew buttercups and daisies," Jenny agreed. "Yes, I'll tell you what I can. I'd love to. What about that muck-spreading? Are you feeling fit?"

It was an old joke.

"She isn't going to do anything of the kind," said Mrs Pilgrim indignantly from the front, and the two girls exchanged glances and laughed.

They received a wonderful welcome at the farm and Esmeralda came to welcome Drina almost at once, as though he recognised her for his mistress.

"Isn't he handsome?" asked Jenny's aunt. "I've brought him up for you, Drina. It's a pity you can't have him with you."

"I couldn't at the flat," Drina said regretfully. "At school we can have small pets if we like – some of the younger ones have guinea-pigs and hamsters and things like that. And there are about nine ponies. But I don't know about cats. I expect he'd miss the farm now. Wouldn't you, my beautiful Esmeralda?"

"Auntie calls him Merry," Jenny explained. "You can't call a great male cat Esmeralda – it's idiotic! Have you ever seen the ballet yet?"

"*La Esmeralda*? No, though one company does part of it."

"Let's unpack and go and see what changes there are!" Jenny cried eagerly, and Drina obediently put down the purring cat and followed her friend to the room they always shared. It had tipsy floors, a window in a gable, and a huge, thick black beam above the beds.

"Such a lot has happened since I was here last!" Drina remarked, looking out into the blossoming orchard. "I've been to Switzerland, and acted in the play, seen several new ballets, and gone to Chalk Green."

"Nothing ever happens to me," said Jenny placidly, beginning hastily to throw her possessions into the drawers. Drina, turning to watch, could not help laughing.

"Oh, Jenny! If Matron saw you she'd have a fit. Underclothes *here* and shoes *there*!"

"Your matron is nothing to do with me. Where are my jeans? I'm going to milk, so I may as well be dressed for it, even though Mother says I'm getting too fat for trousers. I've grown out of my old breeches."

They ran off together to inspect the farm and then later, while Jenny milked, Drina sat dreaming on a corn-bin. It was quiet in the cowshed, except for the faint hum of the milking machine and the occasional clang of a bucket. The sun shone in through a small window on to Jenny's bright fair hair, as she sat peacefully milking a cow that was almost dry and not worth putting the machine on. There was a smell of hay and cattle food, and Esmeralda was washing himself in the doorway, one sleek grey leg raised gracefully aloft.

"A sort of cat arabesque," Drina thought. "They're really much more graceful than ballet dancers."

Afterwards she and Jenny went the rounds of the hen houses to see if there were any eggs, and the late afternoon was so beautiful that it struck at Drina's heart as the wood near Chalk Green had suddenly done. The light was so sharply golden, almost glittering, a cuckoo was calling beyond the orchard, and when she buried

her nose in the waxen flowers of the cherry blossom they had a faint, delicious fragrance.

"Not missing London tonight?" Jenny asked and Drina shook her head.

"Not really, though I think I shall always feel it's my own place. And spring in London is heaven, too, Jenny. Pink May trees in Green Park. I remember them last year. Crocuses in Bloomsbury Square and daffodils along the Mall. Then in the evenings there's a sort of blue light over the buildings: not a bit like the winter light——"

"Anyone would think you were born within the sound of Bow Bells!" said Jenny.

"But I was. Well, not literally, I suppose. But I was born in Chelsea. My parents had a flat there. Jenny, I do sometimes wonder what my father was like. Do you know, it seems unbelievable, but I've got a grandmother and perhaps aunts and cousins in Italy. Granny won't talk about them much; I think she isn't keen on my getting to know them. But she *did* say I'd go to Italy some time. It would probably have been this year, but for Australia."

"Are your relations in Milan?"

"My grandmother lives there. But the family really comes from Rome. Think of it! That's why I'm so dark and my father was as well. Granny said once that the Milanese aren't usually so very dark. And Emilia isn't very. She comes from Genoa."

"Don't go and *live* in Italy, that's all," said Jenny, making her way through a surge of brown hens who hoped that she was going to feed them. "Here you are, Drina! Three lovely warm brown eggs. Don't drop the bucket whatever you do, dreaming about Italy."

"I'm not and I won't," Drina said. "I'm quite happy

to be here at the moment."

"So you ought to be!" Jenny retorted and they returned to the farm whistling *To be a Farmer's Boy*.

The weather continued to be glorious and Drina and Jenny were out nearly all day long. But Drina insisted on practising for a while each morning. This was not very easy at the farm, but Drina managed as best she could, sometimes shutting herself up in the bathroom where the towel rail would act as a *barre*, and sometimes working in the big barn where there was a smooth, clear space.

The farm hands occasionally looked in and grinned at the agile small figure in practice tights and sweater, and Drina's dancing seemed to intrigue Esmeralda who sometimes showed a passionate desire to caper about her feet in the most disconcerting way.

"The angel! He's taking after his name!" cried Drina, but she was forced to carry Esmeralda over to the house and shut him up in the living-room while she practised.

One lunchtime Mrs Pilgrim remarked, "I saw something interesting in the paper this morning. You'll find it interesting, anyway, Drina. The season has started at the Stratford Memorial Theatre, you know, and one of this year's plays is *A Midsummer Night's Dream*. There's been some trouble over the part of Puck. The girl who was going to do it can't get there until May, so someone from the Dominick Company has taken over the part."

"Puck?" Drina cried, much interested. "I thought it was always played by a boy?"

"Not always. Sometimes. I remember once – it's a long time ago – when quite a well-known ballet dancer played Puck at Stratford. Someone from the Sadler's

Wells Company, as it was then. Or it may even still have been the Vic Wells."

"Oh, but who is it this time?"

Mrs Pilgrim groped behind her for the paper and presently pointed out a small paragraph to Drina. "The youngest member of the Company – you see? Bettina Moore. I seem to know the name."

"Oh, yes. She was Little Clara in *Casse Noisette*. That was before she was really properly in the Company. I've always wished I could get to know her," Drina confessed. "She has such a sweet face and she's a lovely dancer."

"Well, perhaps you will one day. There must be opportunities."

"Not for me. Even at the Dominick I'm only an unimportant Junior," Drina said regretfully. "But it's funny! The Company are abroad, and so –"

"If you read on you'll see that the Dominick released her for a few weeks and she flew home."

"*I* wouldn't give up dancing with the Dominick to play Puck!" Drina remarked. "But perhaps she couldn't refuse to help."

"Well, you can go and see this Bettina as Puck, if you like," Mr Pilgrim said cheerfully. "Tickets are never easy to get for the Memorial Theatre, but I believe I can magic up a few. I have friends in Stratford and one of them is connected with the theatre. How would that do?"

"It would be marvellous!" cried Drina. "Oh, I'd love to go! *The Dream* is my favourite play. It was really because of one of Puck's speeches that I got that part in *Argument*. Mr Dominick heard me reading it in class. But would Jenny mind? She isn't keen on Shakespeare."

"No doubt I'll survive," said Jenny. "I'm not being left out, anyway. If I'm bored I can stay and eat ices in the restaurant overlooking the river. It's better than the theatre by far!"

"You dreadful little Philistine!" groaned her mother. "It astonishes me that I've got such a daughter!"

"Oh, you're used to it now," Jenny said casually. "Besides, I do quite like *The Dream*, though there are rather too many fairies flitting about."

"They *dance*!" said Drina, bright-eyed. "I shouldn't mind being a fairy in *The Dream*!"

"Well, do let's go at night," Jenny begged her father. "Matinées are no fun. I like the river when it's getting dark and the lights are beginning to shine out."

By some miracle the tickets were forthcoming for the following Friday. Jenny's uncle and aunt had laughed and said that Shakespeare was not in their line, and that, in any case, they could not get away in time. So the two younger boys were left at the farm in their charge, and Mr and Mrs Pilgrim, Jenny and Drina sped away in the Pilgrims' big car. They had tea in Stratford, at a café with dark oak beams and floors that were even tipsier with age than those at the farm. And afterwards they walked in the flowery gardens by the river.

Drina had often seen the great theatre and had once visited it for a performance of *As You Like It*, but it was a real thrill when they took their seats, excellent ones at the front of the Circle.

Shakespeare was not ballet, of course, but anything to do with the theatre was likely to give Drina a thrill, and then they were to see Bettina Moore whose performance as Little Clara she had much admired. She settled herself with a sigh of deepest pleasure and studied the programme for so long that Jenny glanced at her with laughing despair. She knew full well that her friend was lost to her as long as they were in the Memorial Theatre. Already she was miles away, staring at the curtain.

"Pass Drina a chocolate," said Mr Pilgrim, but Drina merely smiled and shook her head. She never ate in the theatre, not even between the acts, though she and her grandmother sometimes had coffee. In her secret heart she thought it was terrible to need to munch, and so many people seemed to wait until the most moving point of a play or ballet before they started rustling cellophane or silver paper. Drina had a good many views on theatre behaviour by this time and she and Rose had once made a list of all the ill-mannered things that were done around them during a matinée.

Still, the Pilgrims were *not* the kind to rustle and talk once the curtain rose and she knew that the chocolate box would soon be closed until later.

She knew the play well, much of it by heart, but it was astonishing to see it "come alive" on the stage before her. Bettina Moore *was* Puck, a mischievous creature who seemed scarcely real: so light and airy that she was on and off the stage almost in a flash.

"It shows what ballet training will do," said Mrs Pilgrim in the interval. "She really is a delight. Such a perfect body. I've never seen a better Puck. Even the girl I was telling you about hadn't quite Bettina's charm. And her voice is delightful."

"Yes, it's lovely," said Drina dreamily. Bettina's voice was indeed as light and clear as possible. Every word was audible, even when she was moving. It was an odd thing, but she had never heard Bettina Moore speak before, only watched her in the distance, sometimes on stage and sometimes going home from the Dominick rehearsal room in Red Lion Square. "Not all ballet dancers have nice voices."

"They don't need them, I suppose," said Jenny.

Jenny seemed to enjoy the "play within the play" and laughed a great deal at Bottom, but she vowed that the thing she liked best was having coffee in the restaurant. The river looked so lovely in the April dusk, with swans drifting slowly along and lights splashing down on the shining water.

It was a happy, satisfying evening and the words of the play were still ringing in Drina's ears as they drove back to the farm through the deep, dark lanes. "I am that merry wanderer of the night. . . ." Lucky, lucky Bettina, who had been taken into the Company so young and who seemed assured of a career in the theatre. Probably acting Puck was just an interesting experience, as taking the part of Françoise had been to Drina, and Bettina really wanted to be a ballerina. She was not even really a soloist in the Dominick Company yet, for Little Clara had been given to her because she looked so small and young. Mostly she was just in the *corps de ballet*.

"Drina's asleep," said Mrs Pilgrim as they turned into the farmyard and the dogs began to bark.

"She's awake and dreaming!" said Jenny. "Aren't you?" And Drina laughed and admitted it.

"It was all lovely. I enjoyed every moment."

"I wonder if they've remembered to shut up the geese?" said Jenny and they all burst out laughing, Jenny herself included. It was so characteristic a remark, even after a night at the theatre.

8

The Chilterns again

The days passed with astonishing speed after the visit to Stratford, and soon the Pilgrims and Drina were back in Willerbury. Mrs Pilgrim had ordered Drina's summer clothes for Chalk Green at a shop in town, according to instructions left by Mrs Chester, and when the parcel came Drina held up an emerald green swimsuit and three emerald green dresses, with white belts.

"We had scarlet ones at the Dominick," Drina said, parading in one of the new dresses. "I really like red better, but this is a pretty colour, too."

"It suits you," said Mrs Pilgrim, tweaking the crisp, full skirt into place. "I do believe you're getting a little colour in your cheeks! It must be the country air you've had lately. Yes, they're very nice, but you'll travel in your jacket and skirt, won't you?"

"Yes, I think we have to. And dresses get so creased sitting in the train."

So the new clothes went into her trunk, after they had been carefully marked, and Jenny seemed to enjoy helping with the packing, though she had to be restrained from putting walking shoes on top of more delicate things.

"You really are a 'farmer's boy'," said her mother in her usual faintly rueful tone. "Sometimes I wish you were really feminine like Drina."

But Jenny never took offence in any way. She understood her mother perfectly and even had room to spare in her cheerful, contented heart to be a little sorry that she hadn't quite turned out the daughter Mrs Pilgrim would wholeheartedly have enjoyed.

"I'm sorry. I *am* a clumsy idiot sometimes. But even Drina's walking shoes might belong to a fairy. Size twos! And I take sixes. But at least I can sew the nametapes on her new pyjamas. I suppose those are going in the overnight case?"

"Yes. In case we don't get unpacked till the next day," said Drina, gratefully handing over the pyjamas. She disliked sewing even more than Jenny did. "By the way, I never really thanked you for letting me send your old bike to Chalk Green. I think it'll be fun to cycle in summer, and Rose is sending hers."

"You're very welcome," said Jenny placidly. "I wouldn't have got much for it if I had sold it, even though it's perfectly strong and safe. And my new one is a beauty."

"I liked cycling in Willerbury, but Granny would never hear of it in London."

Drina had enjoyed every moment of the holidays and she felt a great deal more able to cope with Chalk Green. Marianne Volonaise's words had taken root and she was firmly determined to get to know and like the Chiltern country, to read widely, and to develop some hobbies that had nothing to do with dancing. All the same, she began to feel tense with alarm and excitement on her last day in Willerbury. How very, very different it would have been if she had been returning to the Westminster flat and the Dominick School!

She was at least to have a glimpse of London, for she was to meet some of the girls and two members of the staff at Marylebone, for an afternoon train to Princes Risborough. There they would all be met by private bus and carried across the valley and up into the hills.

Rose telephoned in the evening to say that she was catching the three o'clock train, too, and was looking forward to seeing Drina.

"I'm so scared that I could die! I never, never thought I'd go to boarding-school, and if it wasn't for you, Drina, I'd say I'm ill or something."

"Of course you wouldn't," said Drina. "Think of your dancing. I've made up my mind to try and enjoy myself this term. I've really thought a lot about it. It's just wasting months of my life to be miserable and homesick. And perhaps Matron will put us together, as I asked."

"I hope to goodness she doesn't put me with that Christine girl, all the same," said Rose's distant voice. "*You* don't like her, but I'd be downright afraid of her. Mum says to stand no nonsense, and that I'm as good as anyone, but it's all very well."

"Of course you're as good as anyone!" Drina cried indignantly. "In fact, you're better than lots of them. You wouldn't have been given such an important scholarship if they hadn't thought you definitely worth it. There are only a very few scholarships to Chalk Green."

"What's that? Rose panicking?" Jenny asked when Drina left the telephone. "Oh, well, you'll look after her. It's a blessing you've got such a good friend."

Drina perched on the arm of a chair and looked at

her greatest friend.

"It's nice of you. I'd hate it if you were jealous. But there's not the slightest need to be in the world. Rose is nice and I'm very fond of her, but you're you."

"Hum!" said Jenny, pulling a comical face, and they went off cheerfully to spend a last hour with Mark Playford who lived only two roads away.

The next morning Jenny and her mother saw Drina off at the station. It was a cooler morning than usual and rather grey, and Drina felt both sad and uneasy. But she was determined not to give in to her feelings.

"It will soon be the end of July and I'm looking forward to that cottage in Wales."

"It's very close to Snowdon," Mrs Pilgrim said. "In a really lonely place, with not even a shop. You like the mountains, don't you?"

"I love the Alps, and I loved Wales that time we stayed at Porth-din-Lleyn. I saw Snowdon then. It was beautiful."

"Philip's coming home for part of his vacation, so perhaps he'll take you girls climbing. He's done quite a lot, so you'd be safe enough."

Then the train came in and Drina had to say goodbye. "I'll write often, and thank you very much for having me, Mrs Pilgrim."

"It was a pleasure," Mrs Pilgrim answered gravely and meant it. "It feels like having a second daughter; something I always wanted."

Drina had lunch on the train and the journey to Paddington seemed short. She got a taxi without difficulty and it made her feel almost grown up to be looking after herself, instead of being met by her grandmother, though she did feel one sharp stab of homesickness for that calm, well-dressed figure. For a moment Australia seemed unbearably far away, in spite of the loving letters that reached her two or three times a week.

She was at Marylebone in only a very few minutes and there was Miss Crawford, her class teacher, standing near the bookstall with a crowd of green-and-grey clad figures. Rose was standing a little apart, looking forlorn, but she brightened when she saw Drina.

"Did you have good holidays?" Miss Crawford asked, looking with some relief at Drina's much happier face. "But I can see you have. Your friend Rose is glad to see you, I know. Perhaps you'd like to introduce her to the others? I haven't had time yet."

Emilia was there, with a much labelled suitcase, and Hildegarde arrived a few minutes later, with another member of the staff who had met her at the airport. Jacques grinned at Drina in quite a friendly way and said something cheerful and welcoming to the shy Rose, and Ivan Lenovitch, the young Russian, who was now living in Britain, said in his clear English:

"Shall we call you Belle Rose? It is a pretty name."

Rose went pink, but looked pleased. "But Belle Epine isn't so pretty. She's a horrid character, anyway. Meant to be."

"You've seen *The Prince of the Pagodas*? I have only read about it."

"I've only read about it, too," Rose agreed and then it was time to take their seats in the train.

Gazing out at the outskirts of London, so quickly being left behind, Drina thought that it seemed a very long time since her parting with Jenny. She was already back in the atmosphere of Chalk Green and even joining in the cheerful gossip, as well as telling about seeing Bettina Moore as Puck. But when the hills and beechwoods lay on either side of the train and Princes Risborough was only minutes away, she simply could not help regretting London. Determined as she was to like this deep and secret countryside, she still felt an exile and would have gone back to the Dominick, if she had been given the chance, without one thought or backward glance for Chalk Green Manor.

The others, however, were delighted to be back.

"So lovely the woods!" said Hildegarde. "Could there be anything more green than beechwoods in spring? Is it hawthorn then, already, high on the slopes?"

"I don't think so," said Miss Crawford, glancing up at the little white trees in the distance. "I think it's the wind turning the leaves of the whitebeams. They're very white on the underside. But the hawthorn won't be long. In a week or two –"

Then they were leaving the train at Risborough and greeting their old friend the bus driver. Drina and Rose sat together and Rose mumbled anxiously, "Will Christine be there already? I do *hope*, if I'm in Ivory, that she's not still there."

"Oh, bother Christine!" said Drina. "You needn't worry about her. Perhaps she's stayed in Paris. Maybe some ballet school there has snapped her up."

But the first person they saw in the hall was Christine herself, scowling fiercely. "It's all *your* fault!" she said accusingly to Drina, who put down her case and stared at her.

"What on earth are you talking about?"

"That I'm in Markova instead of Ivory. And it isn't nearly such a nice room."

"It's exactly the same," said Drina. "Only at the other side of the house. Do you mean that Matron –?"

"Matron's put the new girl there, because she's *your* friend. I do think it's a bit thick. I shall write and tell my mother and ask her to complain."

"Write away!" said Drina blithely. Somehow she didn't mind Christine a bit, especially if it really meant that they were to be free of her.

Christine gave Drina and Rose a very unfriendly glance and went away muttering about it not seeming to matter at all that some people's mothers had been famous dancers.

"Anyway, why should it?" said one of the twins, as the pair materialised out of the surging crowd. "We wouldn't like her any better if she was related to Fonteyn, Markova and Ivory rolled into one!"

"This is Rose Conway," said Drina and the twins shook hands politely.

"How do you do? Glad you're in Ivory. We did a joyous *pas de deux* when we heard we'd got rid of Christine."

The sun came out as they went upstairs and the long polished corridors were flooded with light. Rose paused at one of the big windows to gaze out at the view.

"Drina! It does feel strange. So much country and so few houses and people!"

The two confirmed Londoners stood side by side, their shoulders touching.

"What's that little hill? It looks like an upturned boat. And there are more hills opposite and so many trees –"

"That little hill is called Lodge Hill. We were on top of it once last term and it *was* rather like standing on an upturned boat. I haven't been to the hills over there.

The others say you can walk and cycle for miles, mostly on top. Perhaps I'll go now I've got a bicycle. And you've sent yours, haven't you? Did you see that big white chalk cross on the hillside near Risborough? It's called Whiteleaf Cross and you can climb up and sit on the arms. It's like a sort of chalkpit when you're there. And someone once said there's a very little cross on Wain Hill – that's really the end of Bledlow Ridge, I think," Drina said rapidly, finding some pleasure, to her own astonishment, in telling what little she knew. "There *are* some houses and cottages, though not very many."

"It's most peculiar after London," said Rose, with a further doubtful glance. "But the trees *are* pretty! I never saw so many before."

After that they had to unpack their cases and get ready for tea. Matron bustled about, looking extremely busy and rather harassed, and she said that most of the trunks would have to wait till that evening or the next morning.

By the time the tea-bell rang nearly everyone had arrived and there was a great deal of eager chattering about holiday experiences. No one paid much attention to Christine's Paris adventures and she looked sourer than ever.

It certainly made a difference to have Rose at her side, but Drina was conscious of a growing melancholy as the meal went on. All this term, and all *next* term – what a long time before she would be back at the Dominick, really in the heart of things again!

Some time later she was flying along a corridor in search of Matron, to ask if she and Rose should unpack since their trunks had been sent up to Ivory, when she rounded a corner and went slap into a tall, male figure.

The encounter was so totally unexpected that she recoiled with a gasp, her face scarlet.

"Oh, Mr Dominick! I'm so sorry –"

Igor Dominick looked down at her with some amusement. "So it's Drina Adams! Back again in exile?"

Drina went redder than ever. It always disconcerted her that he remembered her name, when he quite obviously did not know half the names at the Dominick School, let alone Chalk Green. Miss Volonaise must have told him that she thought of Chalk Green as exile. It was difficult to know what to say.

"Y-yes."

He looked thoughtfully at her, and she did not like to pass on.

"Well, you've got Rose Conway to keep you company now. Seen any rehearsals lately?"

Drina gulped and then met his eyes and could not help laughing. She had never forgotten that dreadful day when he had caught the pair of them standing on a flat roof, looking at the rehearsal of the Dominick Company.

"It was *ages* ago, Mr Dominick!"

"So it was. Well, try and enjoy yourself. Chalk Green's all right, and we don't forget you altogether just because you're here, you know. Have you seen Miss O'Donnell anywhere about? I was told she was up here."

Drina gasped that she hadn't and went on thankfully. But there was a sudden warmth in her heart. "We don't forget you . . ." It was still astonishing to her that the great ones took the very faintest interest in unimportant Juniors, and Mr Dominick had sounded as though he really cared how she felt.

Forgetting the unpacking, she stood at the window,

gazing out into the woods at the back of the Manor. But she saw nothing at all but Igor Dominick's face.

Miss Volonaise and now Mr Dominick. . . . Undoubtedly she would *have* to do well at Chalk Green. She would have to work and dance as well as she possibly could. Anything else would be unthinkable.

BOOK TWO
Ballet Elsewhere

1

A Mascot for Chalk Green

Drina's resolution held and she found herself working with a will. Her tension seemed to have gone and her dancing seemed as good as ever it had been; she even felt that she was beginning to make steady progress. Miss O'Donnell was pleased and mildly surprised, and once she said to Drina after class:

"What was the matter with you last term, Drina?"

"I don't know. I suppose I was homesick," Drina said. "I couldn't seem to do anything right."

"Well, you're making up for it now, and I hear it's the same with your ordinary school work."

Drina went off to change, much pleased. It was true that she was finding it a great deal easier to concentrate and her mind and body felt alive, as they had not done for so many weeks.

"I feel as though I've got my brains back!" she told Rose.

Rose was feeling rather as Drina had done the previous term, with the difference that she had had time to think about the change and was determined to do well. The gift of the scholarship had done much to bolster up her never very robust self-confidence, and in a way she liked Chalk Green, even though it was such a great change from her casual, overcrowded home. She liked the twins, and Hildegarde and Emilia, and had even struck up quite a friendship with thirteen-year-old Ivan.

"Because he called you Belle Rose," said Drina, laughingly.

Rose, laughing also, denied it warmly. "He's nice, but he didn't mean it about Belle Rose. He was just enjoying showing his knowledge of a British ballet. I like most people here, except Christine."

But though Rose appreciated the good food and the pleasant company at Chalk Green she did passionately miss being free to wander in London. Perhaps more than Drina, for she had never spent even a night in the heart of the country before. The few holidays that had come her way had been spent at the seaside. She found the woods oppressive just as Drina had done, and for several nights lay wide awake, missing the traffic and alarmed by the strange night cries of animals and birds.

"Like being in the jungle!" she said to Drina. "Sometimes I'd give anything to go off to the cinema and buy fish and chips for supper on the way home."

But Rose had an eye for beauty and after a week in the May glories of the Chilterns she was beginning to decide that there were things to be said for the country. Already the sweet-smelling hawthorn was out on sheltered hedgerows, wild parsley was white and foaming at the side of the lanes, and the fields were beginning to be golden with thousands of buttercups.

Yes, it was a great deal more pleasant at Chalk Green now that Drina had made up her mind to enjoy her enforced exile, and especially with Rose for a companion, but for the first week or two of term she still found her mind wandering to the Dominick. At four o'clock, when perhaps they were out in the woods taking their afternoon exercise, she would suddenly look at her watch and think, "They'll be coming out into the Square soon – Juniors and Seniors – unless something's kept them late. Queenie and Daphne will be walking together, perhaps with Betty and Jill. Miss Volonaise may be crossing the Square to her car. I wish I could have just one glimpse!"

It was the same in the morning. She would visualise them all streaming across Red Lion Square towards the Dominick, running up the steps and then walking quietly along the hall towards the cloakrooms, past her mother's ballet shoes and portrait.

Part of the truth was, perhaps, that Drina had begun to be a personality at the Dominick, within her own age group at least, and at Chalk Green she was quite unimportant, just a comparatively new girl who was dreadfully ignorant about country things. She got on well with her room-mates and with most other people, but she had not yet stepped out of the crowd. In a way she was very humble and she would have been ashamed to realise that she missed her standing at the Dominick. She just knew that she still felt far from home at Chalk Green, even though she was working so much better and the country was a great deal nicer to be in now that the icy winds of March had given place to what amounted almost to a heatwave.

She suggested to Rose that they should try to learn the names of flowers and trees and perhaps make some drawings of flowers and leaves. At first Rose looked astonished, for flowers so far meant little to her, except on street barrows or in florists' windows.

"But why, Drina? What good would it do? They're quite pretty in the fields, especially when there are masses and masses like the buttercups, but I can't see –"

"But you *will*. I've found a really wonderful book in the library. It's as easy as anything to identify things because you just look through all the pages of pictures of flowers of that colour until you find the right one. Then it tells you all about it in the notes."

"I thought you only read ballet books," said Rose, still rather helplessly. "And plays sometimes."

For, since *Argument in Paris* Drina had found that reading plays was very interesting. She had read a number of Noel Coward's and most of Barrie's, starting with *Dear Brutus* which remained her favourite. "Poor Margaret left in the wood!" she had once said. "How awful to know you didn't really exist. If I wanted to be an actress instead of a dancer I should like to play Margaret."

Now Drina looked at her friend gravely.

"So I did, but Madam said it was wrong to read so many ballet books, and I suppose it is a bit stupid."

"Oh, well, if you really want to –"

"We'll take the flower book out with us and you'll see how easy it is. Those were early purple orchids I found yesterday and a few common spotted ones. There are rare helleborines in the woods, too, but perhaps not till a bit later. And did you know that those strange things sort of half-wrapped in a big pale leaf have lots of names – Wild Arum, and Parson in the Pulpit, and Lords and Ladies –"

"I don't know anything, duck," said Rose, at her most Cockney. "But since I'm in the country p'raps I'd better learn." And she took a book called *Flowers of the Chalk and Limestone* out of the library and studied it diligently, at first to please Drina but gradually taking pleasure in the beautiful coloured plates.

After the hard work of ballet classes and ordinary school it was lovely to feel free for a couple of hours in the afternoons, and for much longer on Saturdays and Sundays. Several times Drina and Rose joined cycling parties that were going quite far afield, to places like Long Crendon and Thame out in the Vale, and over the hills across the valley to Great and Little Hampden and past the Prime Minister's country house, Chequers.

Remembering Miss Volonaise's words Drina began to take an interest in the ancient flint churches that belonged to many remote hamlets, and Miss Crawford, who often accompanied the cycling parties, was much struck by the gradual widening of her horizon and did all she could to provide the information required.

"When that child came she didn't seem to have a thought in her head that wasn't connected with ballet and the theatre," she said to Miss O'Donnell. "Understandable in a way, I suppose, but surely a pity at thirteen?"

"I suppose so," the dancing teacher agreed, with a wry smile. "It's the way it takes some of them. Her dancing's really good, far better than I thought at first. But when they're *too* absorbed I always get frightened and wonder what would happen if, for some reason, they couldn't make dancing their career after all."

"It frightens me, too. We've seen some near tragedies. Not a tenth of the students here will get into the Company, I suppose. Anyway, you should see Drina and Rose with their noses in a flower book, and the others all help. Some of them are very keen."

"Sometimes I don't feel like me at all," said Rose one day as the six from Ivory returned from a scramble on Lodge Hill, where wild candytuft, yellow stonecrop and thyme now made a carpet.

"Neither do I," agreed Drina, but she was beginning to be almost happy at Chalk Green.

Up on Lodge Hill that afternoon, away from the others for ten minutes or so, she had lain with her nose in the thyme and felt a sensation that was entirely new to her. A pleasure in being against the earth, warmed by the sun and possessed by that most secret and suddenly enchanting countryside.

Another day she and Rose, escaping from the others in Wain Hill (the end of Bledlow Ridge that was so sheer above the plain), found, by merest chance, the little chalk splash that was Bledlow Cross. They sat on it in triumph, feeling that no one had ever found it before, while the others laughed somewhere above them and the ground dropped sharply at their feet.

Suddenly Drina sat up straighter and looked about her.

"What's that strange noise? It sounds like an animal!"

"I don't know. It's somewhere below," said Rose uneasily.

"Then we'd better go and see. I hope it isn't some creature in a trap. I couldn't be like Sue – or Joan – when she killed that grey squirrel that was so badly caught in a trap, though I know quite well it was the only kind thing to do." Drina was already slipping and slithering down through the tangle of wild privet and other close-growing bushes that covered the steep slope. Her hair constantly got entangled up and she pulled it painfully away from the clinging twigs.

"*Do* be careful!" Rose begged anxiously from behind. "Shall I call the others? You'll never get up again."

"Then I'll go round the bottom. I think the Icknield

Way is down there. I believe it's a dog or perhaps a fox. It's dreadfully unhappy. Don't bother the others. We can manage, I suppose."

Rose gave a yelp of alarm as her foot slipped on the smooth dry ground and the pair nearly hurtled to the bottom, but Drina got her arm round a fairly strong branch and managed to save them.

"Oh, dear! Now I've torn my dress! Won't Matron be cross? Oh, where is he, do you think?"

"Not at the bottom," said Rose. "Somewhere up here."

"Oh, I do hope it's *not* a trap! Perhaps we should have told the others, but there didn't seem time." Drina was very tender-hearted where animals were concerned and the frantic whimpering was making her feel almost sick.

"He's here!" Rose cried shrilly, from a little to the right, and her face showed dirty and scratched through the tangle of undergrowth. "In a little sort of pit and he can't get out. It's a puppy and he's covered in blood!"

"Oh, *dear!*" Drina said again and struggled to Rose's side. Down in the deep chalky hollow in the hillside was a small black and white body and a pair of frightened, unhappy eyes looked up at them hopefully. "Oh, the poor little thing! I'm going down. I'll hold him up to you and you must grab him and hold on tight in case he's so scared he runs off."

But the puppy was in no position to run. One leg was torn and bleeding and seemed quite useless. He whimpered desperately during the rescue and Drina had to set her teeth. It was useless to try not to hurt him.

"I think it'll be better if I hold him under one arm and you try to pull me up with the other. That might

hurt him less."

Rose pulled frantically at her friend's hot, grubby hand and eventually Drina stood once more on the hillside, with the puppy, silent now, in a more comfortable position against her chest.

"I'll climb up with him. It will be quicker and probably easier in the end. You go in front and take my hand when I get stuck. I can just about hold him with the other."

"But where are you taking him? He ought to see a vet with a leg like that."

Drina gazed at her over the puppy's soft head. "To Chalk Green, of course. I can telephone for the vet, or perhaps one of the staff will. There's a vet in Risborough, I think. He came to see one of the little kids' pets."

"But the puppy may belong to someone."

Drina paused to gaze around. There were a few farms out in the plain but, near at hand, no houses at all.

"They weren't taking much care of him, then. Poor little thing! Afterwards perhaps we can advertise or something, but I'm keeping him *now*. I don't care what anyone says."

She managed to struggle up the hillside, past the Cross and through the thick tangle of bushes to the path where the others were now standing and calling. They greeted Drina's arrival – she was wild-haired and torn and bloody – with shouts of astonishment.

"Oh, Drina! Look at your dress! Blood's simply pouring on to it! Poor little pup! What happened to him? He looks as though he's been in a trap."

"I'm afraid so," Drina said with unusual grimness. "I've got to get him back quickly and telephone for the vet."

"But –" they were used to seeing Drina always immaculate, with shining, swinging hair.

Drina was already setting off at a rapid pace along the path through the woods, with no eyes now for the silverweed and rock roses on the grass in the more open parts. Rose, panting a little, kept up with her and the others trailed behind.

"She looks like – like a Crusader!" said one of the twins, and a similar thought flashed into Miss Crawford's mind when Drina marched into the hall at Chalk Green. She looked fiercely protective, ready to fight for the small rescued animal, who nestled in her arms.

"Oh, Miss Crawford! His leg is badly hurt and he was down a sort of chalkpit. *Please* may I telephone for the vet? And *please* may he stay here? I don't believe he belongs to anyone, and he could be a mascot for Chalk Green."

Miss Crawford hesitated. The mangled leg looked very bad indeed. "I'll certainly send for the vet, but he may say that the poor little thing has to be put to sleep. It might be the only kind thing to do."

"But I'd look after him, if nobody minded. I'd bathe his leg and feed him while he was ill, and afterwards the others could take turns, if they like. I know he couldn't be *my* dog, but –"

"Well, we'll see." Miss Crawford went to the telephone, looked up a number in a list that was on a table below and spoke briskly.

"He'll be here in half an hour," she said to the hovering Drina. "If he says it'll be possible to save the pup I'll ask Miss Sutherland if he may stay here. She'll probably say that we must put an advertisement in the local paper, but it does seem that no one is very interested in him."

"Oh, thank you!"

"Meanwhile, you can go and make him comfortable in the stable buildings. There'll be some clean sacks and I'll try and find an old cushion. I'll bring some warm milk for him, too."

"She really is awfully nice!" said Rose as she, Drina and the puppy made their way to the stables.

Drina and Rose missed tea, but neither minded. The vet was a young, quiet man, who took so long to examine the puppy that Drina felt deeply anxious. He asked for hot water and bathed the leg, then bound it up firmly while Drina held the dog.

"It's a nasty mess, but no bones are broken. I'll come and see him tomorrow. I think he might pull through. He's an attractive little chap. Mongrel, of course, but quite nice-looking."

"Oh, good!" Drina was flushed with relief. She had never cared so much about an animal before. "If he's going to be all right he can probably be a mascot for Chalk Green Manor."

The vet laughed.

"With a ballet name, I suppose?"

"I haven't thought yet, but that would be a good idea. I suppose I'll have to ask the others. Petrouchka might be rather nice. Pet for short."

"Myself I'd call him Patch or Whisky," said the young man as they escorted him across the stableyard to his car.

Permission was given for the puppy to stay at the Manor with the proviso that an advertisement was sent to the local paper, just in case anyone was looking for him. Drina would have paid for the vet *and* the advertisement entirely out of her own pocket money, but Rose and the others from Ivory insisted on contributing.

"Of course we'll help. And it will have to be quite a long advertisement. They cost such a lot nowadays."

The puppy was named Petrouchka, no one being able to think of a better name, though Rose would have liked Hilarion out of *Giselle*, and within a week he was getting about quite well in spite of his bandaged leg. The advertisement duly appeared, but no one showed the slightest interest.

Petrouchka settled down most contentedly to being Chalk Green's mascot and was very likely to be the most spoilt dog in Buckinghamshire. But he insisted on regarding Drina as his mistress, though she resolutely tried to teach him that he belonged to all the others, too. Drina had rescued him and looked after him while he was in pain. That was enough for Petrouchka.

2

The Ballet Film

Far away in Melbourne Mr and Mrs Chester sensed the changes in Drina and were much relieved to realise that at last she seemed to be settling down at Chalk Green. Her letters had always been cheerful, but it was a brave, forced cheerfulness, always more troubling than confessed unhappiness would have been.

Mrs Chester had said little when they received those first short letters at ports of call during their voyage. She was not a sentimental or a demonstrative woman; in fact she found it almost impossible to express her feelings. She had brought Drina up since she was eighteen months old, and she had been deeply fond of her, if not always wholly approving. There were facets of Drina's character that she had fought against since the beginning: the temper, the quick passion, the, as her grandmother thought, slightly unbalanced delights and despairs. But Mrs Chester had struggled conscientiously and had seen some result, though she had had to give in over that biggest thing of all – the immovable, deep-rooted determination to dance. Through it all Drina had, without doubt, seemed as much her daughter as Betsy had been. But when she had to choose between her husband and the child, she had told herself that James must come first and that Drina, who would be fourteen next birthday, was well launched and reasonably able to cope with life. At any rate it might strengthen her to be away from home.

Mrs Chester would never have admitted for one single moment the pain and worry the separation had caused her, however carefully she had reasoned with herself. Chalk Green Manor was an excellent school and Mrs Pilgrim was, within certain limits, a sensible and intelligent woman. In the case of accident or serious illness, she told herself often, it would be possible to fly home and be at Drina's side in a very short time. But that was all very well. Drina had not been ill, but she had so patently hated her exile in the country during those first weeks; was obviously homesick for London, her family and the Dominick.

"I hope I was right to come," was all Mrs Chester had ever said, after reading one of the early letters.

Mr Chester worried much more noticeably, for he was very fond of Drina and more ready to show his feelings, but he was nevertheless enjoying the experience of life in a new country and already felt much better in health.

The letters began to change when Drina went to Willerbury at Easter and it was clearly obvious that she stayed in good spirits even after her return to Chalk Green. It really was astonishing to find that she was taking up new interests and not so "soaked in ballet", as her grandmother had always regretfully thought. There was still plenty about dancing in her letters: bits of news about the various classes and the things that were said by Miss O'Donnell. But there was plenty besides.

The swimming-pool has been filled now, Drina wrote, *towards the end of May. It's very small, but really lovely, just at the side of the orchard and not far from the stable-yard. It's six feet deep at one end, but only two in the shallows. I've never bathed where I can see trees so near. It's lovely to lie in the water and look up at the apple trees.*

Petrouchka is growing now and is quite handsome. He nearly always comes out with us on our walks, but not when we go cycling, though he'd be perfectly willing to run beside us. His leg is quite better and seems as strong as the others. He's a very fast runner indeed, but it would be cruel to expect him to keep up with us. Everyone loves him, but in a way he's mine. The thing that worries me about that is what will happen when I leave Chalk Green.

Rose and I are learning about flowers and trees. There are lots of lovely things here. The Icknield Way is bordered with things like spindle and dogwood and little white-beams, and there's a lot of traveller's joy trailing about. Isn't it a lovely name? Nicer than old man's beard, and, anyway, it's only beardy in the autumn. The twins say it's lovely here in the autumn.

I'm reading a lot, too, and you'll be very surprised, because it's not just ballet books any more. I read a book about Italy last week and I do long to go there. Emilia is teaching me some Italian and she makes Genoa sound so interesting, with its palaces and squares and the great port. I long to see the Mediterranean and some of the villages on the coast. Do you think we could possibly go next year?

It's really very nice here in summer. Rose and I know all the people in the village now, if you could call it a village! And we know the people at the farm and the gardeners here and so on. But I still often think of London. We went up last Saturday to an Art Exhibition and a concert. The

Company is in the provinces just now, after their very successful European tour, so we couldn't go to the Dominick. They're talking of starting an Opera Company, so then there would be something on most of the time, as at Covent Garden. But I don't know if I should like opera, except that there is sometimes some ballet included.

I'm going to stay with Rose at half-term. Miss Sutherland asked Mrs Pilgrim and she said she thought it would be all right. I hope you don't mind? It isn't really half-term, because so many of them have nowhere to go, but we can stay away Friday to Monday if we like.

Mrs Chester did mind slightly, for she was a snob at heart and Rose's home was shabby and rather overcrowded. But she had told Mrs Pilgrim to make her own decisions and Drina was too old not to choose her own friends. Besides, it had to be admitted that Rose was a well-mannered girl.

Drina was, in fact, very thrilled about the coming weekend, though she was a little sorry not to see Jenny. She and Rose planned to visit some of their favourite haunts and perhaps even call in at the Dominick on Monday morning. The Dominick half-term had been the previous week, so everyone would be there.

That would have been pleasure enough, but then something happened that made it especially important to go to London. Drina picked up a London paper one day and glanced through the plays and films that were showing. At what she saw in the bottom right-hand corner, she turned perfectly white and her heart seemed to stop beating for a few moments. A cinema in Tottenham Court Road was showing a film called *The Breton Wedding*, with Elizabeth Ivory: "Don't miss this opportunity of seeing a revival of this wonderful film.

One of the few full-length British ballet films, featuring a very great dancer in her most famous role," said the caption.

Fortunately Drina was alone in the common room or her peculiar appearance would have occasioned a great deal of comment. She had never known there *was* a film of *The Breton Wedding*. It seemed like a miracle, utterly unbelievable. To see her own mother dance!

"But why didn't I know? Why haven't I read it in some book? Granny should have told me, but then she might never have expected it to be shown again."

She was perfectly composed when she sought out Rose.

"Rose, we've got to go and see a film during our weekend. Look! I've just seen it. *The Breton Wedding* – the whole ballet, I suppose."

"Elizabeth Ivory!" Rose stared at the advertisement. "She's been dead years and years."

"Yes, I know," said Ivory's daughter calmly. "Twelve years. It's a very old film. I never even knew it existed. Rose, will you come?"

"Of course," said Rose readily. "It ought to be wonderful, even if it *is* old. I've never seen *The Breton Wedding* danced."

"No one of our age has," said Drina. "It's not been done since she died. Don't you remember? No company will do it because it's thought to be unlucky."

"I'd forgotten. She danced in it and then went off in a plane that crashed, didn't she? It was her own special ballet. Oh, of course we must go to see Ivory."

"Are you talking about the film of *The Breton Wedding*?" asked Miss O'Donnell who happened to be passing. "I'm going up myself on Saturday to see it. Actually I saw it when it was first shown and it seemed wonderful then, even though some critics didn't care for the way it was done. The way the cameras were placed and so on. We did talk of taking some of you up to town especially, but decided against it. Anyway, as you're going to be in town there's no difficulty for *you*. Even if the film technique certainly won't seem so good as we expect nowadays, it will be an experience for you to see Ivory."

From then on Drina thought much about the film, counting the days until they went to London. They travelled there with a member of the staff and a few of the pupils who had relations or friends to visit, but then went on alone to Rose's home at Earls Court. Mrs Conway and Rose's sisters and brothers gave them a great welcome and exclaimed in astonishment over their healthy appearance.

"Well, I declare! I scarcely know you both! Who'd have thought our Rose could have got such a colour?"

"It's all that country, Mum!" said Rose, grinning. "Farm smells and woodland smells: you just breathe them in. Never a bit of smoke or dirt. Do you mind? We want to go to the cinema tonight. We'll go to the first showing and be back about nine."

"Do as you like," said Mrs Conway easily. "You can't have seen many films in that lonely place."

Though Drina had longed so much to see *The Breton Wedding*, she found, as they left the Tube and walked towards the cinema, that she was now almost afraid. It seemed so strange to be going to see her own mother for the first time and it would have been a comfort to tell Rose, but she didn't do so.

There was a fairly long queue and they recognised several girls from the Dominick.

"They're taking a party tomorrow afternoon," one

girl told them. "Ivory! Think of it! Mr Dominick says it ought to have been revived ages ago. We're coming again tomorrow."

They moved slowly into the stuffy gloom of the cinema and the programme began with two cartoons. Rose laughed once or twice, but Drina could not even have said what they were about. She was waiting in a state of hungry tension for the ballet film. By the time it came she could hardly breathe. The titles flashed on the screen: "*The Breton Wedding*, with Elizabeth Ivory and Luigi Corotti. Music by the Dominick Orchestra." And then the long list of the cast. Amongst the members of the *corps de ballet* was the name of Adele Whiteway.

"How extraordinary!" murmured Rose. "I wonder if she'll see it, Drina? It must be unbearable to see yourself dance when you can't any more."

And for a moment Drina herself was lost in thoughts of her friend who had been unable to dance since an injury to her leg. "She's in Scotland," she murmured back. "And she really does love her designing."

But it was Ivory whom Drina waited to see, sitting now in an extraordinary stillness, quite unaware of the crowded cinema, the hot, smoky gloom.

It was a three-act ballet, as Drina knew very well, having read about it in many books. The first act was during the Festival of the Blue Nets in an ancient fishing-port on the Breton coast, when all the fishermen danced, first alone and then with the young girls. At first Josette was not there; then she appeared from the door of a little gabled house. Soon she had a long *pas de deux* with the fisherman she was going to marry.

Drina reached out for Rose's hand and did not even

know that she had done so, though her friend's hot fingers closed on her own quite as a matter of course. Rose was thrilled to see Ivory dancing and supposed that Drina was, too. But she naturally never dreamed of the turmoil in Drina's heart and mind.

The second act, which in the film ran on without a break, was the wedding, when Ivory looked so young and unbelievably beautiful. Her arabesques were, Drina thought, the most perfect thing she had ever seen. She had not dreamed, in spite of the good, and even wonderful, dancing she had sometimes seen, that ballet could be a thing of such breathtaking elegance. It came out strongly even in this modern ballet, and she thought with sudden bitter sorrow that Ivory's Aurora and Odette-Odile must have been even more perfect. It was terrible to know that the dancer on the screen was nothing but a phantom and that she herself could never, never see anything more.

The ballet ended with the storm and the non-return of the fishermen. Josette's last solo was a miracle of perfect dancing, the personification of tragedy. The music, based on Breton folk tunes, tore at Drina's susceptible heart and she felt tears splashing down on her dress. She mopped them up hastily, but she was still much moved when they emerged from the gloom into the hot grey streets.

"Let's go this way!" And Drina turned quickly down a side street. She was almost running and Rose had difficulty in keeping up with her.

"Drina! What is it? What's the matter?"

Drina hurried on until she was suddenly brought to a standstill by finding herself in a quiet cul-de-sac. She had scarcely noticed where she was going. She stood there, facing Rose who was almost frightened by now.

"Rose! Oh, Rose! You don't understand. I didn't know I'd feel like this!" She gulped. "I never meant to tell you, but I'll have to or I'll burst. Rose, she's my *mother*. I've just seen my mother for the first time."

Rose began to be convinced that Drina was delirious. "What do you mean?"

"Elizabeth Ivory. She was my mother. Miss Whiteway knows, and Jenny and her mother and Mr Amberdown, but no one else and you're not to tell a soul."

Rose leaned weakly against a wall and stared at her friend's wide dark eyes and scarlet cheeks. "It can't be true! Why, you'd – you'd have told Queenie when she went on about her mother being Beryl Bertram – And when Christine –"

"It *was* hard, but I don't want them to know. I'm going to succeed on my own. Somehow I will. Rose, after – after seeing that dancing I know I've got to do it. Somehow – somehow I'm going to be great and famous, too. I'm going to dance Josette. It wouldn't be unlucky for *me*. One day I shall do it!" For a moment she was transformed into a creature of certainty. She seemed to grow taller as Rose looked and there was a strange likeness to the great dancer they had just seen, though actually Ivory had been a redhead and Drina's looks came from her father.

Rose was silent for fully a minute.

"Oh, Drina!" was all she could finally say.

Drina began to walk again, the way they had come. Already the splendour and certainty were fading.

"Oh, I'm tired! And hungry. It's been the strangest evening I ever remember!"

3

The Dominick in Liverpool

"**I**f you're so hungry," said Rose, after a few minutes, "we'd better go and have some coffee and buns. But we mustn't be very long, or Mother might start worrying."

"I could eat a hundred buns!" Drina vowed. "It's been an exhausting evening."

With her confession to Rose and that sudden flash of future knowledge, Drina had grown quiet and peaceful, and now it was Rose who was excited and disturbed. Over the coffee and Chelsea buns she insisted on hearing the whole story, and Drina told it rapidly, from a day that she just dimly remembered. She must have been about five, she thought, when she first danced consciously.

"I was being a leaf in a twilit wood and Granny was really upset and annoyed. Yes, I remember it was my birthday and she made me stop dancing, turned off her radio and took me to see the candles on my cake. After that I think I always knew she was peculiar about dancing. Perhaps I never would have danced if I hadn't gone to a new school when I was ten and met Jenny Pilgrim."

Rose listened to it all in wide-eyed fascination,

especially to Drina's account of that wonderful night when she went to the Royal Opera House for the first time to see *Daphnis and Chloe*, and she and her grandmother met Mr Colin Amberdown in the interval.

"I nearly fainted when he told me the truth. He had to take my coffee. After thinking that my mother must have been in the *corps de ballet* of a rather bad company it was just too much."

"And you've never *told* anyone?" That, to Rose, was the unbelievable thing, and she was never to be able to understand it. She was not a boastful girl, but she knew with absolute certainty that if *she* had learned that her mother had been perhaps the greatest dancer of all time she would have shouted it from the housetops.

"Only just those few I told you about. And Miss Thorne knew, of course, when she was my chaperone during the rehearsals for *Argument*. She knew my mother. Of course, it might easily have come out, because I sometimes called myself by my real name in Willerbury – Andrina Adamo – and Daphne might have read in a book somewhere that Elizabeth Ivory was married to Andrea Adamo. But I think she's forgotten that I'm not plain Drina Adams, and I hope that Miss Selswick has forgotten, too. That was why Miss Whiteway took me to the Dominick audition, in case anyone recognised Granny. She used to take Betsy about when she was young."

"Betsy? Oh, your mother!" And Rose felt the need of another cup of coffee, even though she was always short of money. "I *can't* get used to it! You had that wonderful weapon to squash Queenie and you didn't use it."

"I'm obstinate. Granny always says so," said Drina,

with a grin. "I'd made up my mind not to tell and I stuck to it. Though I must admit that there've been plenty of times when I wanted to roar it at the top of my voice."

"But," Rose said slowly, "if you'd told the people at the Dominick from the beginning you need never have feared anything. They'd have treasured you and helped you just because you were Ivory's daughter. There'd never have been the slightest chance of them turning you down. You've always been afraid, just as we all are. You're afraid now that you won't get into the Company, or into some other Company."

"I know, but I can't help it. I *won't* tell just to make things easy. I wouldn't feel it was me doing it. If I'm bad, then I must face up to it. I'd have to sooner or later, if I were bad and they *knew* I was Ivory's daughter. If I'm good enough I'll get there as Drina Adams."

"I think you're very, very brave," Rose said. "Far braver than most people. But I really think you're silly, too. When *will* you tell them? Would you if you thought they were going to chuck you out?"

"*No*," Drina said sharply. "I would *not*. Because then I'd have failed and it would be too late. Rose, don't say such awful things! It's true – I *am* afraid. Even though –"

"You've no need to be, really. You do dance well, and you sometimes seem to have something special. Perhaps it's personality. You had it in *Argument*. That was why all those critics liked you and noticed you. I think you're safe."

"If only I could believe it!"

"Well, unless you grow like a beanpole or break all your legs. When will you tell them, then?"

"I don't know. Some day. If it doesn't come out

before, perhaps the day *after* I've danced my first ballerina role, if I ever do. Or I might wait until I feel I'm ready to dance Josette. Only that might look like a publicity stunt and I shouldn't mean it to be."

"Oh!" Rose still stared at her in awe. "Perhaps I'll be in the *corps de ballet* the night you dance Josette."

"I may never get beyond the *corps de ballet* myself and in most moods I feel I'll be content with that."

"Oh, no, you won't!" Rose said positively. "You're not an easily contented person." She had been looking back over her friendship with Drina and suddenly asked, "And Hansl? Your cat mascot?"

"Yes, he's special. That's why I treasure him so. Mother forgot him when she left the Dominick that last night. He wasn't with her on the plane. Granny got quite cross when I started to be superstitious about it. I've got a pair of my mother's ballet shoes as well, and photographs and newspaper cuttings. Granny gave them all to me nearly eighteen months ago."

"Well, I'll never get used to it!" And Rose jumped up. "We *must* go home."

"You promise you won't tell?"

"Cross my heart. Of course I won't. We'd better go by Tube: it's quicker."

After half-term the weeks seemed to pass very quickly. The corn was high and pale in the Chiltern fields and here and there were great scarlet splashes of poppies. The beechwoods were heavy and green and during their walks Drina and Rose found many a rare flower.

"Oh, I do adore summer!" Drina said over and over again, lying perhaps on the hot short grass high above the plain or lazing in the hedge beside a field of silvery barley.

Rose adored it, too, and both had almost given up yearning for London, though it was always a pleasure to go up for a concert or an exhibition. They had not seen the Dominick Company for a long time, as it had been touring on the Continent and was now on an exceptionally long provincial tour. But early in July a busload of the older students were taken to London to see a Company from Paris.

"But I miss the Dominick," said Drina. "The Paris people were awfully good and I thought that *Romeo and Juliet* was splendid, but the Dominick is specially our own."

"They'll be back in September," said one of the twins. "There's that short season before they all fly to Australia for two months."

"But September is years away. The holidays come first."

Holiday plans were certainly occupying most of their minds and Rose was almost the only one who did not expect to go anywhere. She was therefore especially thrilled when her mother wrote to say that they had decided that a week's holiday could be managed. Where would Rose like to go? To Southend? Or perhaps to a holiday camp?

Rose wrote back promptly to say that Southend no longer held any appeal, and not a holiday camp, please. She begged for them to go to Rye because Drina had said it was so lovely.

"There's the marsh and such a lot of interesting places. Oh, Mum, you'd like it when you got there. And we can all bathe at Winchelsea Beach, which Drina says is quite near, or else get the bus into Hastings."

So Mr and Mrs Conway, who would greatly have preferred the cheerful companionship of a holiday camp, agreed. Rose was altering, and if she wanted Romney Marsh and rosy-red Rye on its hill, instead of a promenade and a pier, she must have them.

"I just hope they'll like it," Rose said guiltily. "But I couldn't bear Southend now."

"I hate ordinary seaside places," Drina agreed. "But I do love the sea. I wonder if we can go to Porth-din-Lleyn from Snowdonia? I should love to see it again."

Drina was beginning to treasure unspoilt country. She had now been several times into the Southern Chilterns where there was almost nothing to spoil the perfect symmetry of hills and woods and "bottoms". The cottages and farms seemed to have grown out of that flinty soil – they fitted so perfectly into the landscape.

"To think that once I didn't like the country!" she cried, after a long and strenuous cycle ride to Maidensgrove Scrubs and Bix Bottom, past Turville and Turville Heath and the lovely, hilly park at Stonor, where the great house dreamed under the slopes and deer wandered under the trees. "I never knew it could do so much to you. Sometimes I feel that I want to hold these hills in my hands – they look so satisfyingly curved."

"You do say odd things," said Rose. "How *could* you hold them? But I do love the bare, downy parts along the Icknield Way towards Ewelme."

"Ask your family to take you on the Downs near Lewes in Sussex. You'd love those."

Christine was going to Yugoslavia with her parents and, as one of the twins said, she might have been going to Siberia the way she talked about it. As far as Christine was concerned no one had ever been to Yugoslavia before, and that regardless of the fact that there was a girl from Dubrovnik at the top of the school, a good dancer soon to be transferred to the Dominick School, when she would have to live with foster parents.

Iliska was no more fond of Christine than most people and she shrugged when someone said she wouldn't be able to avoid a meeting with her. "Oh, but in summer we go to our villa on one of the islands. If Christine were nicer I would invite her to visit, but as it is –"

Hildegarde was going home to Freiburg and then to the Bavarian Alps, for she had an aunt who lived in Mittenwald.

"It will be so lovely. We climb and swim in the mountain lakes. And there are gentians and autumn crocus. I wish you could see it, Drina."

"I've only seen the mountains of the Bernese Oberland," said Drina.

"They are higher and more splendid. I love our Alps. You should see the *alpenglow* on the Karwendal and go by train up the Zugspitze."

Emilia, too, was going to the mountains, for her family had rented a chalet in the Dolomites, and the twins were going for a cruise in the Mediterranean.

Listening to all these wonderful plans Drina was sometimes a little sorry that she was not going abroad too, but Wales was, after all, a different country and the peaks of Snowdonia were real mountains, even though they were not so high as the Alps.

Mrs Pilgrim had suggested that she should take Petrouchka with her, but, though Drina would have liked nothing better, she had had the courage and good sense to refuse. Petrouchka could never be hers, for she would certainly return to London before many more months had passed. He was Chalk Green's dog, whatever he thought about the question of mistresses, and he was better in his own place. Chalk Green Manor was never deserted in the holidays, and the gardener was very fond of him, in any case. Petrouchka often spent hours at his cottage on the edge of the woods.

"It wouldn't be kind," Drina told the dog one day and Petrouchka gave her a bright, intelligent look. It really was almost as though he understood. "You mustn't like me too much. I can't have a pet, you know, because we aren't allowed to in our flat and, anyway, you'd be miserable in London."

Breaking-up day came at last. Drina's trunk had been sent off to Willerbury and she was only taking to Wales those things that she was likely to need; sandals and walking shoes, jeans, shorts, blouses and summer dresses. A stout raincoat, too, and two warm sweaters in case it was cold in the mountains.

She was to travel to Willerbury quite early in the morning and the Pilgrims were meeting her at the station at the start of their journey. One of Jenny's brothers was going to a school camp and would join them in Wales later, and another was going away with a school friend for most of the holidays. So there were only the two youngest boys and Jenny.

"And I suppose there'll be Philip?" Drina asked a trifle apprehensively when the first greetings were over and they were speeding north-west out of Willerbury.

Jenny laughed.

"He's arriving at the cottage some time this week. Don't say you're scared of Phil, Drina?"

"A bit," Drina confessed. "He's nineteen now, isn't

he? That's grown up. And learning to be a doctor –"

"He always was a bit big for his boots," remarked Jenny. "But for goodness sake don't let him know you're scared of him."

"Of course I won't," said Drina, with dignity. "But I've got no brothers and it makes a difference. You can't really understand when you've always had five."

"Once it was only three," said Jenny. "I remember Donny and Bill being born – just about."

It was evening when they approached the mountains and Drina drew in a sharp breath when she saw the peaks and ridges of Snowdon against the bright sky. It had been a perfect day and it was going to be a wonderful sunset. Llyn Gwynant was in the shadows as they climbed up the long valley, but higher up the sun was shining still and the air was sweet with mountain smells.

"I came up the other day," said Mrs Pilgrim, "so everything's ready for us. We'll only have to light the lamps and cook supper and get to bed."

"Lamps!" said Drina dreamily. "It sounds so nice and cottage-y."

"It can be a terrible nuisance when they smoke. But no one's ever bothered to put in electricity. It's a dear little house, though. You'll love it. And the view – all that great Snowdon horseshoe!"

The cottage was on the lower slopes of Moel Siabod, facing, as Mrs Pilgrim said, the Snowdon group directly. In that light Y Lliwedd looked stark and wonderful and the peak itself – Y Wyddfa – soared up into the golden air.

"We'll go up to Llyn Glaslyn tomorrow," said Jenny who had been studying the map.

So once more, as Drina stood by the open door

looking across to the mountains, Chalk Green seemed very, very far away and even the ballet world didn't seem to matter so much. They were going to climb, and paddle in mountain lakes, and perhaps go down to the sea to bathe. It was a glorious prospect and she was happy to be with Jenny once again. That night they talked for a long time in their little room with the view of the mountains and the long, deep valley, and, even after Jenny was asleep, Drina lay listening to the sound of a tumbling stream.

When she crept to the window the peaks were dark against the stars and the sweet hill scents came to her nostrils.

The days passed by in almost complete contentment. The house was small, and when Philip came he camped on the hillside at the back, seeming perfectly happy in his tent. At first Drina was shy of him, but she soon got used to his rather lordly ways and there was no doubt that he could be both kind and funny. Sometimes he made her and Jenny laugh so much that they were almost helpless with mirth.

Philip knew and loved the Welsh mountains and with him they made several quite stiff climbs, though of course there was no question of rock-climbing. Drina would have been delighted to learn, however.

"It looks so easy, really, and I'm sure I've got good balance."

"You may have, but it isn't easy," Philip assured her. "I'm quite certain that Mother wouldn't agree. Wait until you're both older."

Drina, already brown from the summer in the Chilterns, was soon as dark as a gipsy, but Jenny did not sunburn easily and was always suffering from a peeling nose and arms.

"It's a dreadful cross to bear! I look a sight and *you* look simply wonderful."

"She's really not bad-looking," Philip agreed condescendingly. "But she is terribly thin and leggy. However, I shouldn't be surprised if she isn't quite striking one day."

"If I were Drina I'd strike you *now*!" Jenny retorted. "She's really nice-looking, and you know it, my boy!"

"Oh, *do* stop arguing about my looks!" Drina begged and went rapidly down the slope ahead of them, splashing through a stream with scant regard for getting her feet wet. Gone were the days, she was sure, when she would have caught cold. The weather, in any case, was wonderful: blazing sunshine day after day. Drina seemed to be under a happy spell, loving the mountains and her companions – even Philip.

It was quite a shock to her when Mrs Pilgrim said one say, "We've got a surprise for you, Drina. We got seats a while ago for a matinée in Liverpool and it's on Saturday."

Drina looked startled. "What sort of matinée?"

"The Dominick!" Jenny cried. "Didn't you know they were in Liverpool for two weeks? We thought you'd be thrilled to the marrow."

"Oh, I am! I am!" Drina assured them. "I *did* know about Liverpool. I saw it in *Ballet Today*. But I had no idea it was near enough and ballet has seemed rather far away, somehow. What are they doing on Saturday? It seems ages and ages since I saw them."

"*Les Sylphides, Petrouchka* and *Gala Performance*."

"*Oh*! I've never seen *Petrouchka* and I do so want to. Thank you very, very much!"

"It will mean quite an early start," said Mrs Pilgrim,

pleased by her delight.

Philip was to look after the younger boys for the day and they were speeding towards Capel Curig by half past nine. Drina hummed some of the *Giselle* music to herself as she sat with her hair blowing. It was wonderful to be on holiday with Jenny and to be going to see the Dominick Company again. Everything was wonderful . . . life was wonderful. It was wholly good to be alive.

They had a picnic on the way and then sped on towards the crowding buildings of Birkenhead. Neither Drina nor Jenny had ever been through the Mersey Tunnel and it was quite a thrill.

"Another new experience," said Drina contentedly. "Oh, Jenny, you don't *mind* seeing ballet, do you?" And Jenny, laughing, said that she thought she could just about bear it.

"But Father's not coming. He's going to visit a business friend and meet us in the Adelphi Hotel for tea."

The moment she stepped into the huge Circle of the Empire Theatre it was the mountains that seemed unreal to Drina. She was back in the world that she thoroughly understood and that held the greater part of her heart, in spite of her growing love for places. She looked round her with satisfaction.

"What a lovely theatre! I do love these huge plushy places and it must be a really big stage. Oh, if only I could go behind and see them all in their dressing-rooms and warming up on stage before the curtain goes up."

"Go round in the interval. They'd probably like to see a Dominick student," Mrs Pilgrim suggested casually.

"Oh, I couldn't! I don't know any of them. I simply don't count."

Immediately the Chopin music started Drina fell under the familiar spell. In some ways *Les Sylphides* was the ballet that was most dear to her. She felt that she could never tire of it, never cease to take delight in those white-clad figures on the blue-lit stage. Her whole being seemed to move with the music; it really was almost as though she was down there with Catherine Colby as she danced so lightly and elegantly on the big stage. Elegance was her great quality and Drina admired her deeply.

Petrouchka was a wonderful new experience, but she felt that she needed to see the whole ballet again to take in the full shape and meaning. There was so much: so many characters at the Fair, so much colour and movement. When the ghost of Petrouchka appeared on top of the booth for a moment at the end of the ballet she gave a deep sigh. How could anyone ever learn it all, remember it all? And yet it was so satisfying to think that if she watched ballets for years, and danced in them also, there would still be more to see and learn.

She enjoyed *Gala Performance*, but in a much more lighthearted way. Even so she was still rather lost as they came out into the sunlit stretch of Lime Street and she only fully came back to earth as they entered the great lounge of the Adelphi Hotel, where Mr Pilgrim was already sitting at one of the tables reading an evening paper.

"Was it good?" he asked, and Drina answered fervently:

"It was wonderful!"

4

Autumn Term

Drina was very quiet during the return journey, but they were all tired and her absorption passed almost unnoticed. But when she was still quiet the next morning Mrs Pilgrim began to be worried. Later that morning she saw Drina sitting alone on a rock, staring at the Snowdon peaks with such a strange expression that she grew really alarmed. What was going on in the child's head? It was a responsibility, after all, to be in sole charge of someone so finely balanced – perhaps a future great artist.

She walked quietly over the springy grass and Drina jumped when she saw her. She rose to her feet, standing poised on the rock, the wind blowing her green dress against her bare legs.

"Drina, my dear, what's the matter?"

Drina hesitated. But her thoughts needed expression and after a moment she burst out:

"It's all so beautiful! *Look* at those peaks and that great sweeping ridge! Look at the lake and the trees and the bog cotton blowing all silvery down there, like little rabbits' tails! But I don't want any of it if I can't have dancing. It's terrible – I know it's terrible – but I'd sooner be dead if I can't dance. Nothing, not even lovely places, could ever make up to me for dancing."

Mrs Pilgrim, far from being reassured, was appalled. What could she say in answer to such passionate certainty? Drina was looking over her head, straight at the peaks still, and her brown hands were clenched.

"But, my dear child, who says you can't have dancing?"

"No one, of course. But something might happen, even just not being good enough. I couldn't bear it. I should shrivel away if I found I could never be a dancer. I don't suppose you understand. Granny would be very angry with me. She says I'm far too emotional. But I mean it. Every word. I should want –" And she stopped.

"Your grandmother is an excellent woman, and I know you're very fond of her, but she doesn't know what it's like to feel utterly dedicated to something."

"In a way I think she does," Drina said shakily. "She's dedicated to *me*, and I keep on doing and saying things she doesn't want or like. Oh, Mrs Pilgrim –"

"Well, I do understand. It alarms me very much to hear you saying such things, but if you're *thinking* them you had much better *say* them – once, at least. If the worst did happen you would have to find the courage to bear it. People don't find dying all that easy. But it won't happen. You'll follow your mother and be great and famous."

"Sometimes I'm sure of it and sometimes not. There's just no telling –"

"Of course not. Anything might happen. But you've a good chance of getting the thing you want and were born for. So forget it, my dear, and go to the farm with Jenny. I want some more eggs and milk."

Drina nodded and leaped off the rock, but Mrs

Pilgrim was left feeling disturbed.

"I really think she would die if she couldn't dance," she said to her husband later.

"What nonsense! You're getting as emotional as the child," Mr Pilgrim said briskly. "She'd do something else. The world is full of interesting jobs. Anyway, she'll probably marry young and have a family. She's only a child still, but even our superior Philip seems rather taken with her."

"She's fourteen in October and she's grown up a lot lately, though I agree she's very young for her age in some ways. Quite unlike Jenny, who knows most things and will always be able to come to terms with life. Perhaps it's just as well, after all, that I haven't got a dancing daughter."

"If it causes all this worry I'm sure it is," he agreed. "All Drina's doubts and ambitions will probably fade away when she falls in love with a handsome young man."

"Don't you believe it!" said his wife, with great force. "That'll just be an added trouble and worry. She's single-minded and she knows exactly what she wants. She may marry some time, but marriage will probably always come second."

"Rotten prospect, then!" said the downright male. "I hope it isn't Philip."

"I hope so, too. But he'll probably fall in love and perhaps marry long before Drina's grown up. Except that his training will take so long and he'll be so short of money. I wish I could see Drina's future just for a moment."

"Why not come and help me to clean the car?" her husband suggested. "I can't go back to Willerbury tomorrow with it in its present state."

"I wish you could stay with us all the time."

"Sorry, but I must get back to work. But I'll be back here again two or three days before you have to leave. And for heaven's sake don't worry about Drina's future."

She shrugged and laughed and followed him out of doors.

By afternoon Drina was herself again, happy with Jenny and the boys. After all, she had told herself while she waited for Jenny at the farm, it was fun to be thirteen and in Wales. Fun to paddle and bathe and climb and to know that, for the present at any rate, all was well.

Jenny was in love with the remote little farm on the mountainside and would gladly have spent many hours of each day there, but there were always so many other things to do, so many plans, that she could never get all the farming she wanted.

When Drina told her something of what she had been thinking, and about the conversation with her mother, Jenny sighed and laughed.

"I do know how you feel. If I were more temperamental I'd be agonising just like you. If I can't go farming when I'm older . . . or at least marry a farmer . . . Oh, yes, I can sympathise, but it's funny that we're such poles apart in our desires. One so down to earth and the other so far up in the clouds. A dim, twilit world!"

"You always say that," said Drina without rancour. "But it isn't really dim and twilit. It's a world of hard work and terrible uncertainties and disappointments."

"And wonderful rewards – I know. There's a move to deglamorise ballet and I try to do it myself, but in my heart I can see its fascination. It's one of the most romantic professions in the world, even in *spite* of Sunday travel and sore feet, and landladies in provincial towns, and having to look like a sylphide when you're feeling bilious or your father's dying. It's the glamour that makes it seem twilit, but it's hard to explain. I only know that the things that matter to me are things growing in the earth, and animals mating and having healthy young ones, and milk production and cattle food – everything about a farm."

"You could have a farm of your own without marrying a farmer," Drina pointed out, not for the first time.

"I know, if I could raise the money, but I don't believe I'll manage it. There are so many of us to educate and clothe and all the rest. There'll be no money to buy me a farm. I can only pray that I meet the right sort of young farmer and that we can be properly partners –"

"But it's years away. I don't want you to marry and grow staid and stodgy. I like you as you are."

"Fair, fat and fourteen!" said Jenny. "Oh, well – race you to that boggy bit!" And they rushed away over the rough ground, laughing and shouting and forgetting, in their pleasure in the sun and the mountain country, that they had ever wondered about their futures.

Throughout the holidays Drina received quite a large number of cards and letters from her friends at the Dominick and Chalk Green. Rose wrote regularly and Drina was relieved to know that the holiday in Rye had been a success. Rose had been enchanted with the old town and with the great spreading marsh, and apparently the other Conways had been happy, too.

Lena Whiteway, Miss Whiteway's niece, sent a card from the Lake District, where she was enjoying some climbing and hill-walking, and Adele Whiteway herself wrote from her flat in Westminster where she was now busy again on designs for a new ballet. Hildegarde sent a beautiful card from the Bavarian Alps, a view of the Karwendal Range near Mittenwald, and Emilia wrote from Italy to say how lovely the Dolomites were and that Drina must certainly go one day. The twins sent identical cards – they really were almost one person and once more Drina thought that it was quite uncanny – and Christine, astonishingly, sent a card from Yugoslavia.

"Just to let you know she really went," said Jenny unkindly, for she had heard all about Christine's much vaunted holiday.

"Maybe, but I don't know how she got my address."

In her turn Drina bought and sent off many pictures of Snowdon, including one to the gardener at Chalk Green, saying that she hoped Petrouchka was happy and well.

The last part of the Welsh holiday simply flew by. Mr Pilgrim returned in time to take them for one or two more car trips, as he had promised, and Drina was thrilled to go back to the strange country of the Lleyn. Once more she saw the little cottages of Porth-din-Lleyn crouching along the shore and she and Jenny climbed up on to the smooth grass of the headland. The sea was dark blue and sparkling, there were coloured boats in the little harbour, and the mountains were blue and clear.

"I shall always love it especially," said Drina. "Dear little place!"

Then at last they were on their way back to

Willerbury for a few days of shopping and packing. Jenny needed new school clothes, since she had well outgrown everything she had worn the previous winter, and Drina also needed various things, though she had hardly grown at all.

"What happens this term?" Jenny asked on their last night together. "I know you're looking forward to seeing autumn in the Chilterns, but is there anything special?"

"Only the Dominick matinée, I suppose," said Drina, sitting on her suitcase to help it to shut. "You know, the show that the two schools give just before Christmas."

"I know, of course, but I'd forgotten. Last year they did *The Golden Fawn*, but you weren't in it because of *Argument*."

"I do so long to dance at the Dominick Theatre, even for one afternoon," Drina said dreamily.

"Well, perhaps you will this year. Why not?"

"But not everyone can. Only a few boys and girls from each class get picked, and it depends on what roles there are. I wonder if we'll do *The Golden Fawn* again? It was a great success. I did manage to see it, because there wasn't a matinée of the play."

"I bet you do get chosen. And then there'll be Christmas."

"Yes."

"You'll come back to *us*, of course, if your grandparents aren't back?"

"Granny says they simply don't know yet," Drina explained. "Grandfather is finding plenty of business to attend to and they haven't booked a date to come home yet. She seems to think it may be January, at the earliest. I do so want to see them again, even though I may be sorry to leave Chalk Green."

"I should think you'd be mighty sorry. What with the country, and Petrouchka, and Rose."

"Yes," Drina agreed thoughtfully. "I shall mind leaving Rose, but she's only got a two-year scholarship to the Manor. No one stays much after their fifteenth birthday and she'll be fifteen a year next December. She's tons better already. She doesn't look the same girl."

The next morning Drina went off quite cheerfully to London, where she once more met Rose and some of the others at Marylebone. It was true that now she was fond of Chalk Green and it seemed almost the most natural thing in the world to find herself going back to the Chiltern beechwoods, the lovely old Manor and all her friends and acquaintances. Petrouchka gave her an enraptured welcome, and Ivory had been redecorated, along with most of the other bedrooms.

"To think that I ever hated being here!" Drina said at tea-time, looking round at all the familiar faces and at the familiar woods beyond the big windows, as yet quite untouched by the bronze and gold of autumn.

She was thinking the same a day or two later as she ran through the woods with Petrouchka before the 'character' class at half past one. She was so lost in her pleasant thoughts that she didn't see Marianne Volonaise until she was almost up to her and then she stopped abruptly, pink and confused.

"Oh, I'm sorry."

Miss Volonaise was leaning against a tree, looking thoroughly relaxed. She smiled at Drina.

"We seem fated to meet in the woods!"

Drina had known that she was at Chalk Green for lunch, but she had never expected to see that elegant figure so far away from the house. The earlier meeting had seemed, ever since its happening, something she had dreamed.

"I was just giving Petrouchka a run. He loves company. But I'm due at my class in ten minutes and I've got to change."

"Well, explain that you were talking to me. I gather," and the intelligent dark eyes searched Drina's face, "that you're happy here now?"

"Oh, yes, Miss Volonaise, I love it. I do think of London sometimes, and it will be fun to be back, but I've learned a lot of things —"

"I'm sure you have, and you look in splendid health."

Drina grinned. It was difficult to be shy, somehow, though the others would have been startled to see her talking so easily to anyone so important.

"Some of my tan is Chalk Green, but most of it is Snowdonia! I was in Wales for six whole weeks."

"And now you're ready to work again? I had a letter from your grandmother yesterday and it seems you're definitely to return to the Dominick in January. If they're not back in England, you're to go to Miss Whiteway for a short while. Did you know?"

"No. Granny wasn't definite in her last letter. So this is my last term here?"

"It is, so make the best of it. Chalk Green has a lot to be said for it, even if you thought of it as exile at first. January will see you crossing Red Lion Square again and perhaps curtsying to Elizabeth Ivory's ballet shoes!"

Suddenly Drina really was shy, for Miss Volonaise was referring to an episode that had happened long ago, on Drina's very first day at the Dominick.

"I didn't know that you'd noticed. I – I remember you were coming down the stairs –"

"I notice everything," said Miss Volonaise, smiling in a way that few of the junior students had ever seen. "And you looked such a little dark-haired scrap, so solemn. Better get off to that class. I may look in later."

So Drina ran away towards the house and, once there, changed at express speed.

The Dominick again in January! It was odd what mixed feelings that definite news had aroused. Delight and a considerable sadness – how strange!

"Still, it's a long time till January," she told herself as she hurried along the covered passage to the studios. "Months and months away. A lot can happen yet."

5

Miss Selswick's Ballet

At first the autumn weather was often wet and cold, but October was only a week old before the sun shone again with almost summer warmth and the countryside lay under a mellow golden spell. The woods were turning only slowly, but here and there the hazels were bright yellow and the Icknield Way was beginning to be hung with berries of all kinds – dogwood and spindle, blackberries and rose hips. The trails of traveller's joy had turned into soft grey-white cobwebs, but there were still wild flowers in sheltered places: toadflax and knapweed, scabious and gentians and even a few late poppies.

Then came the glorious blaze of the dying beechwoods. The brilliant trees surged up the slopes beyond the almost white chalk fields and sometimes Drina felt carried away with rapture when she looked at the wonderful colours and curves of the Chiltern scene.

The students were encouraged to be out of doors as much as possible while the good weather lasted, for soon must come winter rain and cold, when long cycle rides would be impossible and even the nearer woods might be soaking wet and deep under mud.

"It's perfect!" cried Drina as the five from Ivory returned home late on a Saturday afternoon. "Look at the blue smoke rising from the cottages and from that gorgeous bonfire. I adore the smell of wood-smoke and bonfires! Someone ought to make an autumn ballet."

"*You* do it," said Rose.

"Some day I might. I often get ideas for settings and choreography, but I expect they'd be all wrong. I don't know enough yet."

But she was learning rapidly. Her dancing had progressed and she was now amongst the best in her class, though there were a few whose technique was better. Drina's dancing varied rather according to her mood. Sometimes she could do no wrong and at other times, for no apparent reason, her body failed to obey her as completely as it might. But she earned some praise and usually enjoyed the ballet classes more than any others.

"You have the most perfect arms," said Rose enviously one day, after a tussle with a difficult movement.

"What rubbish! They're so thin and sometimes they just won't do exactly what I know they should."

"Well, I heard Miss O'Donnell saying to another member of the staff that your *port de bras* could be really elegant."

"*Did* she?" Drina was immediately wildly happy.

"And she praised your *pirouettes*."

"She's awfully nice. I'm glad we've still got her this term," said Drina.

"And when Miss Volonaise took that class last week she watched you a lot of the time."

"She watched every single soul," said Drina, and it was true that Miss Volonaise's eyes had seemed to be

everywhere. She had said with truth that she noticed everything. "But it was so – so stimulating to be taught by her. She's never taken a junior class before that I know of."

"I think she has occasionally, but not us. She's far too busy to teach much and it was an honour. All the same, she *did* watch you."

"Then I hope she didn't think me too dreadful," said Drina with genuine humility.

Towards the end of October they were all taken up to

London to see a visiting ballet company from the Continent and there were other trips to art galleries and concerts, both part of the Dominick training. Drina especially loved the music of Mozart and Beethoven and one of the concerts had given her great delight as the programme consisted of the overture from *The Marriage of Figaro*, Mozart's *Piano Concerto in D Minor* and Beethoven's *Pastoral Symphony*. She was learning music too, of course, and never found practising a trouble or a bore, but Rose, though her dancing was extremely musical, much disliked her piano lessons.

"I like to listen, not to have to play myself. I'll never be any good." But she had to keep on with her lessons.

News came occasionally from their friends at the Dominick and early in November Rose received a letter from a girl called Lorna that she read out to the others in the common room.

"Just listen to this! *'Everyone's beginning to get worked up about the Dominick matinée now, of course. They'll be starting rehearsals very soon and we're all hoping for a part. The Seniors are doing their own ballet, and perhaps a divertissement, and ours (yours too, of course, because you always join in) is to be a ballet by Miss Selswick. Everyone looks up to her frightfully and she's really awfully nice, though a bit awe-inspiring. Daphne says she always was, only more so, perhaps, when she had her own school in Willerbury. I suppose Drina knows her, too? Well, she's been working on a ballet for us and it's called* The Changeling. *Daphne says she did a simpler version of it at her own school once, but now it's much longer and more ambitious. It's said, but with what truth we don't know, that this time there's going to be a sort of general audition for parts at the Company rehearsal room, not just in class. Anyway, we'll soon know now.'"*

Drina had listened with wide eyes and tightly clasped hands. "*The Changeling*! Oh, but – I loved it so!"

"Did you know it? Were you in it?" A small, interested crowd had gathered.

"Oh, yes. I was to have danced the name part. It was a lovely part," said Drina, suddenly dreamy. "I got it because I *looked* just right – so little and dark. All the others – the brothers and sisters – were fair. But it was dreadful – I got mumps on the very day and someone called Cherry danced instead. It took me months to get over the disappointment."

"How awful for you! I wonder if you'll get the part this time? You ought to," said one of the twins.

"Only a few from our class will get chosen," Christine said jealously. "And they'll give the best parts to the Dominick lot because they're on the spot. It's always difficult for us to get up for rehearsals, though we can practise the dances here, of course. I don't see why Drina should get a part *at all*."

"But certainly she will," said Emilia who had grown to admire Drina very much. They were good friends, and Drina had learned quite a lot of Italian during their walks together.

"Wait and see," said Christine sourly.

Very soon after this conversation it was learned that Miss Selswick and Miss Volonaise were coming to watch the classes at Chalk Green to choose who were to go to London for the audition for *The Changeling*. Quite obviously the whole school could not go, so both at the Dominick and Chalk Green a preliminary choice was to be made.

Excitement caught Drina by the throat every time she thought about it. She longed with all her heart to dance on the Dominick stage and her longing had increased since she had heard about *The Changeling*. The memory of it, though her own part in the ballet had been lost at the last minute, had always held a tinge of magic. There was something so fascinating about the idea of the fair little sister disappearing, stolen by the fairies in the wood, and a dark changeling being left in her place.

Instead of being held first thing in the morning, the ballet classes were staggered throughout the afternoon, so that the visitors from London could see everyone dance.

They arrived in time for lunch, together with the secretary from the Dominick School, and during the meal everyone was more silent than usual because of Miss Volonaise and Miss Selswick at the staff table.

"I can't eat a thing!" Rose vowed and did indeed make a poor attempt to eat the excellent roast beef.

Most of the others sympathised with her and Drina, too, only picked at her food.

"By tea-time we shall know all," said Hildegarde, rather dismally. She yearned quite as much as everyone else to dance at the Dominick matinée, but, though she was a good dancer, she was rather lacking in confidence and rarely did her best on important occasions.

When Drina and her contemporaries arrived in the studio for their class the visitors were there already. Marianne Volonaise, wearing a slim-fitting black dress and a striking brooch, was leaning against the radiator and Janetta Selswick was talking to the pianist. When she swung round her eyes met Drina's.

"Hullo, Drina, my dear! How are you?"

"Very well, thank you, Miss Selswick," Drina

answered, suddenly shy. In actual fact she felt very far from well, for excitement was making her almost sick.

The class started and Drina felt better the moment her hand touched the *barre*. It was so often like that. But, all the same, it was difficult to forget the watching people and the secretary with her notebook and pencil.

Presently Miss Volonaise told them to stop and put on their cloaks.

"You will have heard that the ballet chosen for this year's matinée is one by Miss Selswick called *The Changeling*. When the dancers we choose today come to London she will tell you the story. You know already that only a very few from each class can hope for a part, and perhaps not everyone who comes to London will get chosen either now or later. It doesn't necessarily mean you're a bad dancer. The parts are limited and some of the main ones can go only to fair people. Now Miss Selswick will tell you whom we have chosen to come to London on Saturday."

Janetta Selswick took the list and paused for a moment before she read out the names. There was a deep hush and in it Drina could hear Rose breathing heavily. They exchanged looks and then both glanced at Christine who was standing a little apart, striking an attitude, with her cloak falling back from her shoulders. Quite obviously she expected to be chosen, and she was right, for her name was the first to be called.

"Christine Gifford, Rose Conway, Joan and Sue Meredith, Drina Adams, Emilia Riante . . ." And two or three more.

Drina and Rose clasped hands ecstatically and Hildegarde gave a perfectly audible groan. Miss O'Donnell smiled across at her.

"Never mind, Hildegarde. Perhaps next year. And

you aren't the only one, dear."

After that the visitors departed, the centre practice went on, but Miss O'Donnell knew that she would not get the best possible work from them that afternoon. They were all longing to get away and discuss the choice.

"I could have died with relief!" Rose cried as they changed back into their ordinary clothes. "And you looked as white as a sheet, Drina."

"You needn't feel too relieved yet," Christine remarked. "There's still London."

"So there is for you, too, my girl!" said someone who had not been chosen, but Christine tossed her head.

"They'll remember that my mother was in the Dominick Company."

"Sometimes I wonder why you don't tell her who *your* mother was!" Rose mumbled to Drina. "How you can keep it to yourself I can never understand!"

"It's getting to be a habit," said Drina and they ran off to find Petrouchka who had been somewhat neglected that day.

On the Saturday morning Drina packed her little case, putting in her practice clothes, two pairs of shoes, a towel, and, last of all, Hansl. She could not possibly go without her precious mascot.

Everyone else who was going to London was very excited and lunch was especially early for them. The bus was at the door well before one o'clock and they sped away through the wintry countryside. For the woods were almost bare now, all the brilliant leaves having fallen in a gale a couple of nights before. Now they lay amongst the smooth grey trunks, adding to the russet carpet that always spread over the beechwoods.

It was strange to go into the company rehearsal room instead of into the Dominick School, and when they streamed into the cloakrooms some of the Dominick pupils were already there. They changed hastily and hurried up into the huge light room where most of the Dominick ballets had been born. Jan Williams, sitting on the radiator, leaped off to greet Drina and Rose and his young cousin Bronwen, who had also been amongst the first choice of dancers.

"There you are! I was sure you'd come. How's life in the country?"

"It's fine," said Drina. "But we're not in our normal spirits at the moment!"

"No one is," said Jan, grinning. "Everyone's all het up and Daphne is just about ready to scratch everyone's eyes out. She says she was Selina, the youngest sister, when the ballet was done in Willerbury or wherever it was and doesn't see why she shouldn't be again."

"I don't suppose that's anything to go by," Drina said soberly. "And she's grown a lot and isn't so fair. Her hair has gone quite mousy. But I hope she can be Selina if she wants it so much."

"I wouldn't waste your charity on her," remarked Rose. "She never has a single charitable thought where you're concerned. She would sooner see you out on your ear than with any part at all."

"I always hate the jealousy," said Drina, and meant it with all her heart. It had been the thing that troubled her very much since the beginning, in the old days in Willerbury. There were always people who hated you if you got a good part. Much as Drina longed for a part in *The Changeling*, even the most unimportant role, she felt she could never hate Daphne, Queenie or Christine if they were successful and she failed.

Presently they went to warm up at the *barre* and one of the ballet teachers at the Dominick began to take a class for everyone. Halfway through, Igor Dominick, Miss Selswick and Marianne Volonaise entered the room and stood talking in one corner. Then they turned round and stared with such concentration at the dancers that Drina was not the only one who felt nervous. It really was most nerve-racking!

Finally the class stopped and Igor Dominick said, "Well, this isn't an audition in the full sense of the word. We can't ask you to do any of the dances from *The Changeling* because only one or two of the classes at the Dominick have learned them yet. But we have a good idea of your capabilities, and we know just how many dancers we want, as well as, in some cases, what they must look like. Miss Selswick wants to tell you the story of the ballet."

Janetta Selswick smiled round at the anxious, intent faces.

"The setting is a woodland glade, with a cottage on the right. In the cottage lives a woodcutter, his wife and their eight children – four boys and four girls. They are all extremely fair and the youngest and fairest is called Selina. These children love to dance in the wood, but they are forbidden to dance there after sunset, because then the fairy folk are likely to be about. But Selina is very wilful and she likes nothing better than to skip out after the others have gone to bed and dance by herself in the moonlight. She has another reason, too. Once she met a little Prince from the nearby Castle and she always longs to meet him again.

"Well, in the first act we see the brothers and sisters dancing. Then, as it gets dark, their parents call them in. As soon as they have gone to bed the fairies and elves appear and dance briefly, hiding themselves when Selina peeps out of the cottage and then comes out to dance. As Selina dances she is surrounded by fairy folk and, in spite of her protests, they bear her away and leave a changeling in her place – a strange little dark child, who is utterly different from fair Selina.

"In the second scene it is morning again and the changeling is dancing alone in the glade. The brothers and sisters find that Selina has gone and that there is a dark stranger in her place. Everyone is very upset, for the changeling is mischievous and alien, but they don't know how to get Selina back. They see her dancing with her fairy captors but cannot reach her. And the changeling just laughs and dances wildly on her own when Selina is carried off for the second time.

"In the third scene the Prince is wandering in the wood by moonlight and sees Selina dancing with the fairies. He manages to separate her from them and dances with her, and this breaks the spell. The fairy folk ask to have the changeling back, but she is rather reluctant to go, having enjoyed being a mortal child. She, the Prince and Selina dance together, but in the end she has to go, dancing away after the fairy folk, while the woodcutter, his wife and the brothers and sisters dance round the Prince and Selina.

"That's the gist of the story and the dances are really very simple. The brothers and sisters will wear pale colours – blues and yellows and greens and pinks – and only the dark changeling will be in a hard, bright colour. Scarlet, to show up her darkness. And now to business." There was not a sound as she began to make her choice.

Two of the oldest students were chosen to be the woodcutter and his wife, and then four fair boys to be the brothers and three fair girls, two of them the Meredith twins, as the sisters.

Drina, standing in anxious tension, could not help seeing Daphne's face and she hoped quite fervently that Daphne would be Selina after all, though it was true that now she was neither so small nor so fair as she had been in Willerbury. But a little girl from a lower class at the Dominick was chosen, a girl called Marita.

Jan Williams was to dance the Prince, it seemed, and now everyone was tense and expectant, wondering who would be the changeling. There were quite a number of small, very dark girls both at the Dominick and at Chalk Green.

"I've given the changeling to Drina Adams," Janetta Selswick said briskly. "She looks the part and is something of an actress as well as a good dancer. It's a simple part on the surface, but it does need a good deal of personality."

Drina could hardly believe her ears. She had never dared to hope that such a thing could happen. To dance the changeling in Willerbury, at a show given by a small dancing school, was one thing. To be chosen from so many to dance the name part on the Dominick stage . . . that was an enormous honour. She felt cold with shock and excitement and she scarcely heard the long list of names of the fairy folk, nearly thirty in all, for the Dominick stage was a large one and there was no reason why there should not be plenty of fairies and elves to give as many dancers as possible a chance. But she did see the faces of Queenie, Daphne and Christine, and some of her wild happiness faded.

When at last they were dismissed to have some tea in the canteen at the Dominick School Drina had to be hauled along by Rose and the twins.

"Congratulations! It's splendid, Drina!" the twins cried, and Rose added her comment:

"You really deserve it and what a blow for Christine! She's only a fairy and Daphne's only understudying one of the sisters. Being a fairy suits me very well, though Mum and Dad will think I ought to have a bigger part, of course."

Drina, hemmed in by her friends, could not get a word in. But the happiness had returned and she longed to dance and sing on the spot. Her only sorrow just then was that her grandparents would not be there. There seemed small chance that they would be home for Christmas.

6

Trouble for Drina

But Drina's happiness did not last long. She saw that Queenie, Daphne and Christine had got together at a table in a corner, with several others who had never been very friendly towards her. They all had their heads together and then glanced up to stare across the canteen.

"They hate me!" Drina said. "Daphne always hated me being the changeling in Willerbury and now she's only understudying – but I can't help it. She could never have the part."

"Of course she couldn't," Rose retorted. "Don't take any notice of her. She's a beast, anyway!"

"But how can I help taking notice of Christine? I have to see her every day. Daphne's not so bad, really, and I don't blame her for minding, but in a way I'm afraid of Queenie and Christine."

"Queenie's a nasty bit of work," Jan Williams agreed. "And your Christine doesn't look much better. They're all having a splendid witches' sabbath at the moment, but maybe it'll get it out of their systems!"

However, the "witches' sabbath" didn't seem to have done anything more than whip up dislike for Drina, so lucky with the name part in the ballet. As Drina and

Rose were going to the cloakroom, Queenie, Daphne and Christine barred their way.

"Look here, Drina! It isn't fair and you know it! Miss Selswick has only given you this part because you had it in Willerbury. She knows you and it's a clear case of favouritism."

Drina, very pale, stared at their unfriendly faces. "It isn't! You ought not to say things like that. Miss Selswick never would – Mr Dominick and Madam wouldn't let her."

"Don't you believe it! It's her ballet and they've given her a free hand. And so dear little Drina is benefiting!"

"I think you're all wicked!" cried Rose, staring indignantly from one to another. "And if it was just favouritism why hasn't she chosen Daphne for Selina?"

"Because she always loved her dear little Drina," said Daphne bitterly.

"If I were Drina I'd go now and say I didn't want the part," said Queenie, her handsome face almost ugly with spite.

"I wouldn't risk making myself unpopular in both schools," Christine contributed. She had only met Queenie a few times before, but they were of one mind over their dislike of Drina Adams. It would, however, have been a different matter if one of them had got a good part and the other hadn't.

Drina, feeling strangely trapped, had nothing to say. Her happiness was clearly in the dust and she had made definite enemies as well.

"If you don't be quiet I shall go and *tell* one of the staff what you say!" Rose said fiercely.

"You'd never dare," said Queenie. "Mousey Rose, who couldn't say boo to a goose!"

"I would dare, then, if Drina won't. I'll go now –"

But Drina shot out a hand and gripped her arm.

"Don't, Rose! You can't tell tales."

"Then will you resign the part? It's the only decent thing to do."

Drina's warm happiness might be a thing of the past, but she felt her temper rising.

"I will not. It isn't true what you say. I'm sure it isn't. Mr Dominick and Miss Volonaise must have agreed. I'm going to dance the changeling whatever you think and say. I'm truly sorry that you haven't got better parts, but you're luckier than some of them, who got nothing."

But the thought of Beryl Bertram's daughter being a mere fairy was very bitter to Queenie. "Far too big for your boots, you've been, since that play last year!"

"If it's a question of the size of boots," said a voice behind them, and Jan stood there, "we might think yours the wrong size, Queenie! Really, you are the end!"

They glared at him. He was not tall, but he had great character and even Queenie was not keen on arguing with him.

"Leave Drina alone. She's a better dancer than any of you, anyhow."

Silenced but not, naturally, agreeing with a word he said, they went off in a bunch and Drina said shakily:

"I don't know what to do. I said I wouldn't give it up –"

"And you won't. The staff wouldn't let you, anyway, without a full explanation. Look here! You and Rose are going to get left behind."

They rushed to put on their outdoor clothes and were the last in the bus, for even Christine was there before them. Drina sat in silence all the way back to

Chalk Green, depressed and troubled. She had got her heart's desire and yet she could have cried.

Most of the unfortunates at Chalk Green who had not had a chance to be in the ballet were pleased about Drina's success and told her so with warm generosity, but there were a few who echoed Christine. It *must* be favouritism, since Miss Selswick already knew Drina and she had had the part in the past. There were plenty of other dark girls who were quite as good dancers as Drina.

Christine was naturally delighted to find that a minority, at least, agreed with her unkind words and thoughts. She had never been popular and had always told herself it was because the others were jealous of her, and it excited her – and helped to make up for her own disappointment – to egg the few unkind ones on to belittle Drina's triumph.

"Don't listen to them!" Rose said indignantly. "It's only half a dozen of them, anyway. Poor silly sheep, following Christine!"

"They're beasts!" said Bronwen Jones with equal indignation. She was a fairy and perfectly happy about it. "We all think you're just right for the part, Drina. And *you* won't suffer from stage fright after being in that West End play."

"Oh, I expect I shall," Drina protested. "Some actresses and dancers always suffer from stage fright, however long they've been in the theatre." She *did* try to ignore the unkind comments, and it should have been heartening that more than three-quarters of the school was delighted by her success, but somehow the poison had settled in her sensitive mind. She would lie awake at night and ask herself if it could be true that Miss Selswick had favoured her for old time's sake.

Commonsense told her that no one of Janetta Selswick's standing and integrity would dream of doing such a thing, and that Igor Dominick and Miss Volonaise would never, in any case, have agreed, but commonsense warred with her troubled doubts.

She grew a trifle pale and listless and found it impossible to take the pleasure in being the changeling that she would have done if there had been no dissenting voices.

Miss Selswick came out to Chalk Green on the Monday morning after the Saturday audition in London and began to teach the dances from her ballet. She taught Drina alone, which was a further annoyance to Christine.

Drina worked hard and she loved the dances from the first. The familiar *Changeling* music delighted her as it had done in Willerbury and the dances were well within her capabilities. But there was no joy in her heart and the fact showed.

Janetta Selswick was vaguely troubled, but to her anxious enquiries about Drina's health she only received the reply, "I'm quite all right, thank you."

"Well, don't catch something at the last minute," Miss Selswick said kindly. "I know that getting mumps that time nearly broke your heart."

"I've got an understudy, though, haven't I?"

"Yes. Mallory O'Shea at the Dominick. She's quite a good little dancer, but she hasn't your acting ability. Don't you dare to let me down!"

So the words that had trembled on Drina's lips, "I don't want to do it after all!" were never spoken, and when the Chalk Green dancers went up to London for the first real rehearsal the ballet took shape surprisingly quickly. But, in London, Christine was supplemented by Queenie and Daphne, and Drina's spirits were very low when they had tea after the rehearsal.

"I can't enjoy it at all," she said dismally to Rose, who clucked angrily.

"I never knew you were so spineless!"

"I'm not!" Drina cried, stung. "But all the time I was dancing they were glaring at me and it saps my – my pleasure in the part. I'm going to be an awful failure and then they'll be glad."

"Well, *I* would be ashamed!" said Rose, with unaccustomed fierceness.

After that there was a full rehearsal every Saturday, and on the third occasion Drina spent the Friday night with Adele Whiteway who had collected her from Chalk Green in her car.

Miss Whiteway had been primed by Janetta Selswick to find out what was the matter if she could, and was much concerned to see that her protegée was so pale and depressed-looking. But she waited until it was almost bedtime, when Drina was sipping hot milk before the fire. Fortunately her niece, Lena, was staying with a friend for the weekend, so they were alone.

"I thought you'd be in the seventh heaven at being chosen. What's the matter, Drina? Are you homesick again? Or not well?"

Drina blinked desperately, but the tears rose to her eyes at the sympathetic tone. "It's nothing. I'm being silly, but – but –"

"You'd better tell me. Out with it!"

So then Drina told her the whole story, not minimising the unpleasantness of Christine, Queenie and Daphne. She ended with a rush, "Do you think I ought to give it up? I do love it so, really. But I hate knowing that they mind so much, and if it *was* sort of favouritism –"

Adele Whiteway said something under her breath as she looked down at the bent dark head and the thin tightly clasped hands.

"Oh, Drina, you are a silly girl! If you're going to get far in the theatre world you'll have to grow a great deal harder, I'm afraid. You'll need an extra skin, my poor child. There'll always be some jealousy and a few people who make themselves thoroughly unpleasant –"

"I know. I've always known. But this time I feel there may be a little truth in it. Because I *was* the changeling in Willerbury, and it's because Miss Selswick knows me that they –"

"Then forget it all. You were chosen because you were the right person in every way, and I happen to know that it was Miss Volonaise who was keenest to have you. Miss Selswick was divided between you and someone else at first – but never mind whom."

Drina's eyes were very bright.

"Really?"

"Yes, really. So don't you dare let us all down by thinking any more absurd thoughts. You absolutely fit the part: I thought so when I watched last week's rehearsal, even though you certainly weren't at your best. So hold up your head and enjoy yourself, and let's have no more of this nonsense."

"You really think it's all right?" Relief was flooding Drina and she looked a different girl already.

"I do, and so does everyone else. I've a good mind to have a word with those wretched girls, though they're not really anything to do with me. On second thoughts, it will be enough if you dance brilliantly and make everybody proud of you!"

"I will! I will! But I do wish that Granny and Grandfather could be there."

"*I* shall be there," said Adele Whiteway. "And so will quite a number of people who are interested in you. Didn't you say that the Pilgrims might come up for the matinée?"

"Yes. Jenny and her mother. Jenny says she wouldn't miss it for anything. She's not a ballet fan, but she was awfully upset when I had mumps years ago and couldn't dance the part."

"There you are, then! Now hop off to bed and be fresh for tomorrow."

So Drina went to bed feeling more lighthearted than she had done for some time. Suddenly *The Changeling* was her own again, to treasure and enjoy in its entirety.

But she was troubled with dreams of not being able to dance, after all, and was glad when morning came.

7

Snow

The heartening talk with Adele Whiteway helped Drina immeasurably and she was a different girl at the rehearsal the next day, with just the right amount of elfin strangeness. Miss Selswick watched her with relief, and Christine, Queenie and Daphne with a good deal of gloom. They knew, somehow, that Drina had escaped from them and was herself again. Their gibes would not matter now; she was lost in the ballet, happy and confident again.

"And a good thing, too!" said one of the twins to Rose. "She does dance well, doesn't she? And she almost *looks* not quite real. As though the fairies dropped her in Red Lion Square!" Which, after all, was a high compliment and Rose triumphantly passed it on to Drina.

After that life was entirely happy again and Drina even enjoyed the country in the winter, though she had hated it so much during the bitter winds of early spring. Early in December the weather turned very cold indeed and the woods were sometimes silvered with frost. The seeded willowherb stood still under the leafless trees, grey-white and tall, and in certain lights the larchwoods were a deep red-gold.

She wondered how she had ever thought the country – and particularly the Chiltern country – dismal and dull, for there was endless delight to be had from the curves of the landscape and plenty of colour, of a muted kind, even on a cold, sunless day. But there was one colour that was not muted and that was the brilliant scarlet of the holly berries. There were also other berries in the Icknield Way to be picked for the big vases in the hall.

Life was very busy, what with ballet classes, ordinary school work and many other interests besides, but Drina never forgot Petrouchka and nearly every day he went for a walk with herself and Rose, or perhaps with everyone from Ivory. Petrouchka had grown into a strong and handsome dog, though he was never to be very big. He loved the walks with his friends, but he was perfectly happy in the woods by himself. He was a great hunter and often worried Drina by disappearing for hours on end, returning muddy and bright-eyed to leave some trophy – perhaps a rabbit or some other small hapless creature – on the back door step of the Manor.

"I do hate the corpses so!" Drina groaned. "But he always looks *so* pleased with himself! I'm dreadfully afraid of traps. They're such wicked things. One of these days he'll go out and not come back."

But Petrouchka always turned up in the end, to be petted and fed by his adorers.

"I shall miss him so," Drina said one day. "But I couldn't possibly take him away to London and he'll be perfectly happy without me, I suppose. He's got eighty-nine other mistresses, after all!"

"But you are the special favourite," said Hildegarde. "It was, after all, you who found him."

So far there had been no definite news of the return

of Drina's grandparents and she was planning Christmas with the Pilgrims in Willerbury. It would be fun, but very different from her last two London Christmases. She knew that she would miss the London scene especially then.

Chalk Green was to break up on the Monday before Christmas and the Dominick matinée was on the previous Saturday. The dress rehearsal was to take place on the Friday afternoon and excitement was mounting amongst everyone taking part. When Drina thought of the actual performance cold shivers ran down her spine, and little thrills of excitement, too. Somehow the matinée seemed more important than all the performances of *Argument in Paris*.

Her scarlet costume for the ballet had been made in the Dominick work-rooms and when she tried it on she was delighted. The brilliant red suited her to perfection, and with it she was to wear scarlet ballet shoes and a scarlet ribbon to hold back her hair. The dresses worn by the sisters were very pretty, too, and the fairies' costumes were delightful: so gossamer fine and sparkling.

The only real worry that anyone had was the state of the weather, for on the Monday of the important week everyone at Chalk Green awoke to a howling north wind and wild flurries of snow; by afternoon the hills and woods were white and the snow was still falling.

"What if we're snowed up?" was the constant cry, and Miss O'Donnell said on one occasion:

"We'll get you there somehow, never fear. If the roads are very bad you'll have to walk to Saunderton station and catch a stopping train. But we'll hope it won't come to that."

"I'd walk to *London* if it was necessary," said Rose loudly, and everyone laughed and told her that she would do very little dancing after such a long tramp.

On the Tuesday the snow had stopped, the wind had dropped and the sun shone on a cold, bright world. Everyone was urged out of doors in the afternoon and the younger ones took great pleasure in building an enormous snowman on the lawn and organising a fierce battle with snowballs. The five from Ivory, with an excited, enraptured Petrouchka, climbed up through the woods until they were on the hill's edge and, looking out across the white, still plain, Drina was filled with such sharp delight that it hurt. How lovely the Chilterns were! Their soft, secret magic had captured her heart so entirely that she knew, more clearly than ever before, how she would miss them when she was back in Westminster. The winter silence of the woods, the brilliance of holly berries, the blue light on the deep banks of snow . . . She stored up many more pictures in her receptive mind.

They went singing home as the sun sank in a blaze of red and gold, their faces glowing under their emerald green caps. Their feet made a crunching sound in the clean hard snow and it was a new hobby to try to identify all the bird and animal tracks.

"You'll be here to see the spring," Drina said to Rose. "The snowdrops and the first catkins and the winter aconites."

"But I shall miss *you* horribly!"

"Anyway, first there'll be the dress rehearsal, and the matinée, and breaking up and the Christmas holidays. Oh, Rose, the matinée!" In the end, in spite of everything, conversation always got back to the important event at the end of the week.

To everyone's dismay it was snowing again on the Friday morning and there was an acute anxiety until the bus turned up to take them to town for the dress rehearsal. But the main roads had been cleared and there was no real difficulty once they had left the narrow lanes on the ridge.

After the white and silent countryside it was strange to find London only lightly touched with snow, though in places there was a deep slush.

"It feels rather like arriving from the moon!" said Bronwen as they left the bus in the car park of the Dominick Theatre.

It was thrilling to stream in through the stage door and Drina was enchanted to find that, for the important occasion, she was to share one of the star dressing-rooms with the girl dancing Selina.

"When *Argument* finished," she said to Rose who was paying an admiring visit before the stress and strain of the rehearsal, "I thought I might never have a dressing-room again until I was quite grown up. Fancy – at the *Dominick*!"

"One of the Seniors has Catherine Colby's dressing-room," said Marita. "You know – the one who has the principal role in their ballet."

"For just two days we can imagine we're the real company," Rose cried and went back contentedly to the large dressing-room she was sharing with most of the fairies.

The dress rehearsal was rather an anxious time for everyone, as such occasions usually are, but Drina enjoyed herself. It was so wonderfully exciting to be on the Dominick stage at last. Her own part in *The Changeling* went off without a hitch and she was flushed and happy at the end, when they took their places in the stalls to watch the Seniors' *divertissement* and ballet.

"If only nothing happens now!" she thought. "I *feel* splendid, that's one thing. No mumps this time!"

Hansl, who had been in the place of honour on her

dressing-table, went back to Chalk Green that night, and they travelled in softly falling snow, so that there were many worried faces.

"If only it would stop!" cried Bronwen. "It's lovely, but if we wake up and find ourselves snowed up —"

"Don't think of it, please!" begged Emilia with such comic earnestness that everyone near her laughed.

In the morning it had clearly snowed heavily in the night, but no flakes were actually falling at breakfast time. But the sky was heavy and grey and there was a sort of mist over the valley. Drina felt uneasy and could not finish her bacon and egg, and Christine looked at her white face triumphantly.

But it was only excitement and Drina felt too restless to settle. Her case was packed, the changeling costume had been left in London and there was nothing to do but fill in time until the bus came for them at about eleven-thirty. They were to have a quick lunch in the canteen at the Dominick School and be at the theatre soon after two o'clock.

She put on her boots and thick coat and went out to look for Petrouchka. There was no sign of him about the buildings and she trudged over to the gardener's cottage. The man met her with vigorous shakes of the head.

"No, Miss. I've not seen him since yesterday afternoon, when I saw him haring off into the woods. He didn't come here last night, though he's been sleeping by the living-room fire since the weather turned so cold. I never gave it more than a thought, I must say. Thought you'd got him up at the house."

"I never gave him a thought, either," Drina said guiltily. "We got back late from London and just had supper and went to bed. Oh, Mr Billing, you don't think he's lost? You don't think he's been out all night?"

"I couldn't really say," said the man. "But he's a born

hunter, even though he's not very big. Maybe he slept in the stables. There's plenty of sacks and straw there and he's fond of the place."

"But I always think of traps –" And Drina trailed off, much upset, and went hastily through the outbuildings; then, taking off her snowy boots, all over the house. No one remembered seeing Petrouchka since lunch-time the previous day.

"This comes of having ninety mistresses!" Drina groaned. "Oh, dear! I wonder where he's got to? The woods are so snowy –"

Rose, it seemed, had been captured by the music teacher for an extra lesson – which seemed hard just before the Dominick matinée – and Drina put on her boots again and tramped across the lawn towards the lower woods. Everyone seemed busy and there really wasn't time to organise a search party. It was already a quarter-past ten and the bus would probably be early because of the danger of slippery roads.

"If he doesn't turn up, Hildegarde will see to it when we've gone," Drina thought as she skirted a deep drift at the edge of the wood. "The rest of them aren't leaving till much later. Perhaps I'm being silly. Perhaps he slept in the stables or in one of the common rooms, and has just gone out again."

It was strange in the woods, so dark and still that she was almost afraid. For the first time since early spring they seemed menacing, frightening. She tramped on along one of the main paths, calling and whistling all the time. Her voice seemed to echo back from the trees, but there was no answering bark. Not even any footprints in the snow to guide her, but then it had snowed in the night and if Petrouchka had been out since yesterday afternoon –

As she walked and called, her thoughts dwelt mainly

on the Dominick matinée. In so short a time now they would be at the theatre and the audience would be taking their seats. The curtain would rise on the woodland scene and *The Changeling* would have a brief reality; something created, made as perfect as possible, and then lost. It was a pity that it had to be like that. She had thought it over *Argument*. The thing that was created just slipped away and was forgotten, except in the minds of a few people who cared enough to remember.

Thinking thus, she had left the main path and was cutting up the side of the ridge. The trees were thicker than ever and the light was very bad. The grey mist seemed to have thickened and she suddenly saw, with a leaping heart, that there were snowflakes on her coat. So it was snowing again! And Petrouchka was lost! And in a very short time she must turn round and go back to the Manor.

Her voice seemed little and lost in the vast silence of the wood and the flakes fell faster and faster, finding their way without difficulty through the bare trees. Standing quite still and looking about her, Drina thought that it was like the setting for a strange winter ballet. It would not be sylphides who emerged from the trees, but creatures stranger and more menacing.

She was just going to give up the search when at last she heard a bark and her heart leaped with relief. Ahead, just visible through the flakes, was a sort of open shelter probably used by woodsmen. And emerging from the shelter was Petrouchka. He was yawning and looked draggled and tired, but his eyes were bright and he seemed delighted to see her. He frisked round her, barking until the woods rang.

Drina bent down in the snow and hugged him.

"Oh, Petrouchka! I thought you were dead or in a

trap! And I believe you've been asleep on that lovely bed of wood shavings. I suppose you hunted until you were worn out and then just crawled in there, naughty, hunting dog! Well, now we must get back as quickly as we can. I can't risk missing the bus."

Petrouchka barked again, then came to heel and looked up at her enquiringly. Drina saw with disquiet that the snow was falling very heavily indeed. The wood had darkened even in the last minute or two, and there seemed nothing in the world but grey trunks and a whirling white mist that began to settle thickly on her coat and hair.

She set off as briskly as she could, but Petrouchka, after a short while, sat down in the snow and gave a loud protesting "Woof!"

Drina stopped and stared at him.

"Come on! What's the matter with you? I'm sure it's the right way. Those are my footmarks, though they're almost filled up already."

Petrouchka "came on", though apparently not very willingly, and in the end Drina picked him up and clutched him to her. To her dismay she saw that her footprints had disappeared and there was no real sign of a path. The one she thought was a track turned out to have a great deal of soft mud under the snow and she floundered in an alarming way. Beginning to be thoroughly upset, she put Petrouchka down again – he was dreadfully heavy to carry – and said sternly:

"Home, boy! Surely a bit of snow doesn't bother you? I thought I knew these woods by heart, but they look different today."

They did indeed, and Petrouchka seemed none too sure of his direction. He ran round in a circle and then set off to the right, floundering in the snow which in places came up to his shoulders.

They progressed for five minutes or so in what Drina thought must be the right direction, since it was slightly downhill, but the woods seemed to go on and on without the slightest change. She had definitely lost the main path and, though she might be heading roughly in the direction of the Manor, she had no certainty of it. Petrouchka, whimpering, was in a drift that came almost over his head and she snatched him out and carried him again. The snow was very bewildering and now she could scarcely see a couple of yards in front of her.

When they came to a group of thick holly bushes in a tiny clearing she stood still in their shelter and tried to think. It was ridiculous to be lost in the Chalk Green woods when she had ranged them from end to end for months! In fact, she *couldn't* be lost! In a few minutes she would find the path and then go on quite easily until she saw the Manor in front of her.

But it didn't work out like that. The snow fell even faster and Petrouchka had definitely decided that he could be of no possible help. The drifts in which they found themselves only bewildered the dog, and he greatly preferred to be carried.

Drina's arms ached and after a time she was forced to put him down again and rest against a tree trunk. Her watch told her that it was already five past eleven and she began to visualise the bus arriving and everyone waiting for her.

She *couldn't* be late! Not on this most important day! It just wasn't possible.

But the snowbound woods were suddenly entirely nightmarish and she began to think bitterly of a fate that, not content with bestowing mumps on her on one occasion, could play such a trick on her now. Chalk Green was probably not far away, but it might have been at any distance for all the fact helped Drina. If only she could get back to the path – any path! – instead of floundering so helplessly. If only Petrouchka were not so tired and disinterested. If he had tried he could surely have found his way back, even through the deepening and fast-falling snow?

"Why don't you try? Oh, Petrouchka, do try!" she implored him, giving him a push in the direction she thought the Manor might lie, but Petrouchka set off the opposite way and, after a few moments, scrambled up on to a fallen treetrunk and sat there with his tongue hanging out and his tail swinging the piled snow in all directions.

"Oh, you *are* idiotic!" Drina wailed, growing more angry and frightened every moment. She had just remembered that her watch was slow and that it must already be eleven-fifteen. Calling the dog, she set off again and, ten minutes later, realised that she must have been floundering in a circle, for here they were back at the fallen treetrunk, with the snow that Petrouchka had displaced already almost restored by the drifting flakes.

She was growing tired as well as frightened, and the snow had long since seeped over the top of her boots. Her woollen gloves were wet and the snow made her eyes smart. She shouted until she was hoarse and no answer came, and at last she faced the truth. It was nearly half past eleven and she was still lost in the bewildering maze of trees. It was the day of the Dominick matinée and she was not going to be there to dance *The Changeling*.

It was the most terrible moment of her life.

8

The Dominick Matinée

For a short time she felt weak and utterly miserable, almost ready to sink down in the snow and give up trying to find the way. But she had read of people falling asleep and then dying in a snowstorm, and it seemed terrible to die at fourteen and two months, with most of her life still before her.

So she set her teeth and ploughed on, sometimes carrying Petrouchka and sometimes, because of his weight, having to make him walk. When next she looked at her watch the correct time was a quarter to twelve and she supposed that the bus must have left without her. On such a bad day they would not dare to wait long, for already the timetable was rather tight. It allowed for only a short time at the Dominick canteen and then a quick journey down to the theatre on the Embankment in time for dressing and making up. If only *The Changeling* was later in the afternoon . . . if only . . .

Thinking thus, Drina pitched down a steep bank and landed on hard snow. The snow had broad tyre-marks on it and there was another bank only a few feet away. It took several moments, all the same, for her to realise that she was in a lane and she had scarcely registered the fact before she heard the sound of an approaching vehicle.

A second later a radiator loomed up, almost on top of her, and she snatched up Petrouchka and screamed as loudly as possible. For it was a green bus – that was clearly to be seen, even under the layer of snow – and the indicator said "Private".

The bus had stopped and the driver was leaning out, shouting indignantly. Then he recognised the Chalk Green uniform, covered with snow as it was.

"My dear child –!"

"Oh, Mr Crump!" Drina cried with infinite relief. "I was lost and I thought I'd never get to London –"

The driver knew her face and voice, and assumed correctly that this was the girl whose absence had delayed their departure.

But before he could speak the door opened and Miss O'Donnell stepped down into the snow.

"Drina, my dear! We've been frantically worried! They're going to organise a search party back at Chalk Green. Where *have* you been?"

Drina felt shaky and strange, but her heart was singing. It was all right! She was saved! It was not going to be another tragedy, after all. After the nightmare time in the woods it was almost too much and she couldn't speak.

Miss O'Donnell pushed her and Petrouchka into the bus.

"You'll have to come as you are, and bring the dog as well. He can be shut up somewhere at the theatre, I suppose. Someone said you'd gone out to look for him and the snow came on so heavily – I'll just speak to the driver."

The bus seemed very warm after the icy woods and

Drina found herself received with wild excitement. Rose cried:

"I brought your case! I was sure you'd manage it somehow and I told the others to tell you . . . Oh, Drina, what happened?"

"I was lost and so was Petrouchka. He just couldn't find the way and we went round and round. Then I fell down a bank and heard the bus coming."

The bus started with a jerk and Miss O'Donnell came back to Drina. "Are you all right, dear? Would you sooner go back?"

"Oh, no, thank you," Drina said clearly. "I'm perfectly all right, only rather wet. And it's rather nice to have Petrouchka with us, because, after all, he's our mascot."

"There's a rug – here it is! Take off your coat and put it in front near the heater. Are your feet wet? Well, take off your boots and tights and put them in front, too. Sit on that seat by yourself and tuck your feet under the rug. Someone lend her a towel and another for Petrouchka. We can get others at the Dominick. Dry your hair, Drina. It's soaking. And we've got emergency rations in case we get snowbound coming back."

Willing hands came to Drina's aid and by the time they were speeding along the main road she was curled up under the rug, rubbing her hair and warmed by a cup of piping hot coffee. The bus stopped at the first telephone kiosk and Miss O'Donnell spoke to Miss Sutherland at the Manor, explaining that all was well and that Drina and Petrouchka were on their way to London.

"I never knew such frightful weather before Christmas!" she said, shaking the snow off her shoulders as she re-entered the bus.

The only face that had not been delighted at Drina's astonishing arrival in their midst had been Christine's, as Drina had noticed at once, even in the depths of her bewilderment and relief. But everyone else seemed wildly pleased and Rose was ecstatic.

"I was horrified! I just couldn't believe it at first. But someone said you'd gone to look for Petrouchka and then, when you didn't come – oh, Drina!"

"Anyway, it's all right now," said Drina contentedly. As warmth flowed through her she was filled with a delicious sense of well-being. Even stage fright was forgotten in her wild relief at being on the way to London.

She dozed a little during the journey and awoke much refreshed and in high spirits as the bus slid to a standstill in Red Lion Square. After that, time passed with astonishing speed. They had soup and sandwiches in the canteen and then were taken to the theatre. It was snowing in London too, but only slightly and the main roads were perfectly clear.

Seagulls were wheeling over the grey river and the wind was bitter as the dancers ran from the bus, across the car park and down the narrow side street to the stage door.

"I can't believe I'm here!" Drina cried as she burst into her dressing-room. Rose, following with Petrouchka, a piece of stout string tied to his collar, agreed.

"Oh, Drina, aren't you scared? The theatre's sold out. Think of it! I know that most of them are parents and friends, but there'll be some members of the Press, Miss O'Donnell says, and quite a few people who are interested in ballet."

"I don't think I'm scared *now*," Drina remarked and, in fact, she felt on top of the world. "Oh, I do hope that Jenny and her mother have got here in spite of the weather! Miss Whiteway's certain to be here, anyway."

She had received several notes and looked through them hastily.

"I thought there'd be something from Granny and Grandfather. A cable, perhaps. But maybe it'll get here later. Oh, Rose, I do love my dress!" And she took it down carefully from its place behind a curtain.

"It suits you marvellously," said Rose and then went off to change into her fairy costume. There was not too much time, for they had to warm up before the curtain rose.

It was nearly a year since Drina had been behind the scenes in a theatre and the whole atmosphere of the Dominick was getting into her blood. It might only be the yearly show by the students, but there was the same bustle as for a real performance. Stage hands hurried along the passages, electricians called to each other across the stage, and presently, the calls went out for the dancers.

But Drina was already on stage, warming up. It was wonderfully exciting to be behind the curtain instead of out in front and she was sure that the audience would be enchanted with the charming set for *The Changeling*.

Then it was two-thirty. Part of the Dominick orchestra had taken their places in the orchestra pit and the lively overture suddenly rang out. Drina ran to the wings and the curtains parted softly to show the brothers and sisters dancing together in the woodland glade.

The Changeling went without a hitch from the first moment. It was very simple, but everything blended into a perfect whole – the lilting music, the setting, the colours of the costumes, and the graceful dancing. Drina was immediately lost, as she had been in *Argument in Paris*. For the time being reality was this corner of the woods and she *was* a fairy changeling. There was applause at her first entry and a great deal more at the end of her first dance. She looked so small and so strangely elfin in the scarlet dress, that the audience, too, almost believed her not quite real.

"She *looks* fey!" said Marianne Volonaise to Igor Dominick, in one of the stage boxes. "That child has great personality and it comes out the moment she gets on a stage."

"And she's a striking-looking kid," said Igor Dominick. "As well as being a good enough dancer for her age. But who's to say – ?"

"No one, of course. She's much too young."

"But she's made a good start. She reminds me of someone. I've thought so often."

"So have I," agreed Miss Volonaise. "But I've never been able to place it."

It would have been a shock to both of them if they had known that little Drina Adams reminded them of Elizabeth Ivory. Not in actual looks – for Ivory had had red hair and greenish eyes – but in some indefinable quality of movement and character. It was nearly thirteen years since Ivory had danced on that very stage and twelve hours later she had been dead, mourned by half the world.

Drina, as she waited within the cottage door during the next scene, did not dream that she was being discussed in the box above her, but she did think briefly of her mother, remembering that it was the Dominick stage that had seen some of her greatest triumphs. When she appeared again for her wild little dance with the alien brothers and sisters, she seemed more vividly alive and her movements were even surer than they had been before.

In one of the star dressing-rooms Elizabeth Ivory's own mascot was on the dressing-table. It was nearly thirteen years since the black cat had been there, on that same fatal night. But no one knew, or were to know for a very long time. If it had got to the ears of even one journalist Drina would have become famous overnight, blazing in some of her mother's glory.

As it was, towards the end of the last scene, she danced away into the woods after the fairies and elves – a changeling who had enjoyed her little contact with earthly people but who was returning to her own place.

Then, after the final ensemble, the ballet was over. The curtains came swishing down, to rise again on the whole group of dancers. Jan Williams, as the Prince, was in the centre of the front row, with Drina and Marita on either hand.

The applause was gratifyingly enthusiastic and Jan, Drina and Marita took several curtains alone. Then someone hissed from the prompt corner, "You alone, Drina!" and she pushed the heavy curtains aside and stood there smiling and curtsying. Some flowers were brought up to her and she took them dazedly. For a moment, so brief a moment, it was like being a real ballerina, not a student from a dancing school. She was rather horrified when tears stung her eyes and she retreated hastily.

Once more the curtains rose on all the dancers and Drina glanced down at the label on the bouquet as she stood there. What she saw made her heart leap, for it was a card in her grandmother's writing: *To Drina, with all our love and many congratulations.*

The house lights were on when Drina raised her eyes and for the first time she looked straight at the front row. For a moment she thought she must be dreaming, for there they were, smiling and clapping, her grandfather and grandmother whom she had thought on the other side of the world!

She went dazedly away to her dressing-room, clutching the flowers, and Rose followed her.

"What is it, Drina? It was wonderful! You were a great success. Don't say you're not thrilled to bits?"

"Oh, Rose, I am! I am! But I've had a shock. I don't think I imagined it! Granny and Grandfather are there, in the front row! And I never knew . . . I never dreamed . . ."

Rose's face flushed and her eyes shone. "I knew. Miss O'Donnell told me. They telephoned last night, but it was to be a surprise for you. They flew home and got to London yesterday. Oh, Drina, if you'd stayed lost in the woods how awful it would have been!"

"But I didn't!" Drina cried and danced down the long bleak passage. "I didn't get mumps and I didn't stay lost! Oh, Rose, when can I see them?"

"I expect they'll come behind. It's the interval now," said Rose, and was right. For, only a few moments later, there was a knock at the door and Mr and Mrs Chester stood there.

9

Out of Exile

It was a joyful reunion. Drina hugged them both and asked questions wildly, tears trembling on her long lashes. Her grandfather looked much moved, but through it all Mrs Chester remained her usual controlled self.

"You did very well, Drina, and we're proud of you. And how well you look, though perhaps it's the make-up. How can one tell?"

"Oh, Granny, did you *really* like it? Isn't it wonderful that I had a chance to be the changeling again? I felt so dreadfully bad that last time. Oh, Granny, was it good?"

"I thought it was very good," said Mrs Chester quietly. "And you danced very well for your age."

No one would ever have known, least of all Drina, that she had been moved almost to shameful tears as her grandchild danced and then took that curtain alone, holding the flowers and looking so starry-eyed. For Mrs Chester *did* know all too well whom Drina resembled, and she had been in the theatre on the night when Ivory danced for the last time. She had fought with every weapon she knew to stop Drina from dancing and it had all been to no purpose. Drina had

gone straight on to that moment when she stood before
the blue curtains, smiling as her mother had smiled.

Mrs Chester had told herself fiercely that this was no
real ballet performance; that it indicated nothing of the
future because a black-haired girl of fourteen danced a

simple role in a children's ballet. But it had been no use. She had been sure, in the depths of her heart, that there would come a day, quite inevitably, when she would be in close touch with great fame once more. She did not want it; she dreaded it, in fact, but fate was going to be too strong. The only child of red-haired Betsy held, she felt convinced, the seed of greatness.

But Drina was not thinking of greatness. Already her little triumph had fallen behind her and she was just childishly glad to have her grandparents back again.

The dressing-room was soon very crowded, for Marita's parents were there, too, and Miss Whiteway, Mrs Pilgrim and Jenny had found their way in.

"We ought to see the rest," Drina said presently. "The *divertissement* will be over, but I'd like to see the Seniors' ballet. There are seats for us in the gallery."

"Then hurry into your ordinary clothes," Mrs Chester said briskly. "We'll go back to our seats and will see you afterwards, for a few moments. Then on Monday –"

"I'll be home! But," and Drina's face fell, "what about the flat? And Jenny? I was going to spend Christmas with her."

Mr Chester, who looked wonderfully well, laughed and Jenny jumped about excitedly.

"It's all arranged, Drina. We can't have the flat until New Year's Day, but we're all going to a hotel for Christmas. The three of us, that is. Then Jenny is coming to stay at the flat on the third of January."

"We knew they were coming," Jenny told Drina. "Mother had a cable two or three days ago. But we didn't tell you, because it was to be a surprise. We'll miss you horribly, but you'll have a wonderful time and it will be fun to see the flat again."

Though Drina had wanted to see the Seniors' ballet she got very little benefit from that seat in the gallery, for her happy thoughts went round and round. Life was so satisfying, so exciting. She thought she had never been so happy before.

The snow had stopped when they returned to the Chilterns and everyone was sleepy after the exciting day. Drina herself gave Petrouchka his supper after all his adventures and made him a comfortable bed in one of the common rooms.

"Oh, Petrouchka, you nearly made me miss this whole wonderful day, but I shall forgive you. I shall miss you so!"

Sunday was spent in last-minute packing and, in Drina's case, in saying goodbye to everyone. For she would not be returning to Chalk Green, except perhaps as a visitor. She did hope to call in and see everyone, including Petrouchka, by the spring at any rate.

"I shall just have to see you all again and the ridge and everywhere! I think I shall often ask Grandfather to drive us this way. I shall always love the Chilterns and all the dear little hamlets. There's one place I never went to: I saw it on the map and wished I could. A little village called Dancers End."

"Only you don't want to 'end'!" said Rose.

The snow was too deep for them to go very far, but the sun shone on Sunday afternoon and they managed to get to the top of the ridge for Drina to take a last look at the snowy plain. The little chalk cross lay deep under the drifts and the bushes were laden with fluffy whiteness.

"I'm not really sad," Drina remarked as they returned to a last tea at the Manor. "It's been lovely and I wouldn't have missed most of it, apart from those awful first weeks. But it will be good to be back at the Dominick, and one day you'll be back there, too, Rose. You're very well, now, aren't you? But a year *is* such a long time!"

The twins and Hildegarde and Emilia were deeply sorry to think that Drina would not be coming back, but relieved that they were to have Emilia's little sister with them in Ivory and not Christine.

"Bianca can speak little English," said Emilia. "But you'll like her and she will love Chalk Green."

"And someone else can have Christine!" said the twins, doing a cheerful *pas de deux* along the corridor.

The next morning the buses were at the door, as well as large numbers of private cars whose owners had braved the wintry weather, and by lunchtime Drina was in London, at the big hotel where she and her grandparents were to spend Christmas.

So it was a London Christmas after all and Drina enjoyed every moment of it.

"I hated going into exile," she said thoughtfully to her grandfather as they walked to the Abbey on Christmas morning. "But I think I've learned a lot. The country is so lovely and I'm more independent. But oh! I am so glad to have you back!"

Mr Chester looked at her for some moments. He was glad to have her alone for a little while.

"Yes, I gather you've had a great many new experiences. And, of course, there'll always be new experiences for you *somewhere*. I shouldn't be surprised if the next ones were in Italy."

It was Drina's turn to stare.

"In Italy? Next summer, do you mean?"

"Well, perhaps not until the summer, but maybe well

before that. We have been in correspondence with your Italian grandmother and she wants to see you."

"To see me?" Drina was very startled. "But I always thought she couldn't be at all interested in me. She's never ever written or sent any presents to me, even at Christmas —"

"I'm afraid it wasn't lack of interest," her grandfather said gravely. "You're old enough now for me to talk to you almost as an adult, aren't you, Drina? Fourteen isn't quite a child."

"Sometimes it seems dreadfully old," Drina remarked and he smiled wryly.

"I never felt so old as when I was in my teens! Drina, there was a quarrel — by letter, mostly, though Signora Adamo did come to England after your mother's death. She was very interested in you then; too interested, your English grandmother thought. She was your guardian and she didn't want you to come under any Italian influences. You must remember that she had just lost a very beloved daughter in the most tragic circumstances and you were all we both had. There was some regrettable unpleasantness and Signora Adamo went back to Italy in a very hurt and indignant frame of mind. Until recently we have heard nothing from her, but just lately there have been letters — quite amicable ones, thank goodness — and the result is that we have agreed to let you visit her as soon as possible."

"Oh, fancy!" Drina was not sure whether to be delighted or dismayed. "I think I shall be scared."

"Not you. You'll love seeing Italy and, after all, you *are* partly Italian. Your grandmother lives in Milan, but there is an aunt and cousins in Genoa and more cousins, I believe, in Rome and other places. So you see why your new experiences are by no means over?"

"Yes, of course." Drina walked on in silence for several minutes. "I'd really love to see Italy and I can speak some Italian. I made Emilia, who shared a room with me at Chalk Green, talk to me."

"Yes, you told us in a letter and it was good news."

"But," and Drina's voice was very definite, "my first important new experiences will be at the Dominick. It will be strange to go back and that comes first."

"I know that the Dominick always comes first," said Mr Chester and his words were almost lost in the sound of the Abbey bells.